Chapter 1

"If we survive this," she muttered, "remind me to kill you."

Elsabeth ought to have found the morning enjoyable. The sun hung high in a clear blue sky, and a warm midsummer breeze carried the rich and fragrant smell of turf through the widely-spaced trees of the wood. Columns of golden light pierced the ceiling of greenery overhead and dappled the road, where lichen, brush, and trailing vines clung to the trunks of the trees. Here and there she caught the silver glint of sunlight on the strands of spider webs, and the grove was alive with the singing of birds.

Unfortunately, the five armed men encircling her spoiled the pleasantness of the morning. Rough faces with shaggy hair and unkempt beards leered at her. They all dressed in heavily-patched homespun wool, with leather boots and belts that were weighted down with pouches and knives. Two of them hefted simple cudgels, likely cut from trees around them. Another leaned on a broad-headed wood-axe, and the fourth carried a tall ash spear. The last, and leader of the band, gripped the handle of what was once a kriegsmesser, likely scavenged from some battlefield. The blade broke a span from the end some time ago, and had a new point and edge ground into the remaining length.

She was younger than most of them, having only seen a score and three summers, and taller, with an athletic frame supported by long and shapely legs clad in dark, woolen hose. Elsabeth's copper hair spilled loosely down her back in a gleaming cascade to just below her shoulder blades, with her forelocks drawn back from her heart-shaped face by a thong of leather. A long coat of brown leather hung open over a red velvet doublet fastened with silver hooks from collar to waist. She wore a rondel in a sheath at her back beneath her jacket, and she flexed the fingers of both gloved hands around the red leather grip of a longsword, its blade a yard and a hand in length, as she regarded their adversaries.

"You worry too much, Tetty," her companion said. He was many years her elder and stood well below the height of her shoulders. Wild and unkempt silver hair framed his portly round face, and a wiry white beard shot with streaks of black was on his chin. His blue eyes were small and round, and the skin around them was heavily lined. A loose ankle-length gown of white wool, well stained by the dirt and grime of travel and spilled ale, disguised the impressive girth of his belly. Over this he wore the black woolen mantle of his order, cinched about his waist with a belt of woven cord. He gripped his arming sword with one hand, and a short carved staff in the other. A battered old buckler of steel hung from his belt. "The King of All will see us through. Have faith, my child."

The chief of the men confronting them glared. "You are about to chat with him face-to-face if you do not return our property to us, Brother."

"Bah! The cheap horse piss you lads passed off as ale has dulled your wits, my son. I am but a humble man of the Wheel come to minister to your souls in these troubled times." The friar glared back and scowled. "I am no thief!"

"Not exactly," Elsabeth said.

2

No Good Deed…

By D. E. Wyatt

No Good Deed...

Copyediting by EbookEditingServices.com

Cover art by Aprilily

ISBN: 0615888038
ISBN-13: 978-0-615-88803-3

For my father, who put Tolkien in my hand and helped start me on this journey.

No Good Deed...

He turned his glare on her. "Be silent, child, I will not take such insolence from you."

She rolled her green eyes and shook her head. "No, but you are only too happy to drag me along on your little schemes, Hieronymus. Why do I even listen to you?"

"Well, I did not see you trying to talk me out of it," he huffed.

Elsabeth turned on him and glared. "I spent all last night, and all this morning, while you dragged me out here trying to talk you out of it!"

"But you did not, because it was a good plan."

"I did not because you are too stubborn to let anyone else put a thought in once you have it in your mind to do something foolish. I only stayed with you to keep you out of trouble."

"How dare you! I am too old to need a nursemaid, girl. I had everything well in hand until you decided to empty your ale all over the head of that lout." Hieronymus waved vaguely at the man standing on the road in front of them. "I was given no choice but to hasten things along!"

The man tightened his hands on the grip of his kriegsmesser and glared "Quiet! B—"

Elsabeth cut him off before he could continue, and stretched to her full height to tower over the rotund friar as she put herself into his face. "If he would have kept his hands to himself then I would not have needed to!"

"You spoiled everything! A few more rounds and we could have just walked out of there, and they would have noticed nothing until the morning!"

"A few more rounds and I would have been left to carry your fat ass all the way back to Friuli on my own."

Hieronymus glared back and shook his staff at her. "I will have you know I could out-drink you even with a ten-round head start, woman!"

"Only if I piss in the tankards to water them down for you first," she snapped back.

"Still your tongues, both of you!" their pursuer cried. "You argue like a bunch of women!"

"You keep out of this," Hieronymus snapped. "This is a matter between me and the girl, my son. Once I have finished with her I will see to you."

"I have heard enough! I want my property returned now. Hand it over and I let you keep your fat head." He turned his eyes on Elsabeth and leered as they wandered the length of her body. "You I may keep a while longer as compensation, after I cut out your tongue."

Elsabeth rolled her eyes and glanced to her companion. "We can discuss this later, but we really ought to deal with them first."

Hieronymus nodded in agreement. "I will have words with you later. Which ones do you want?"

"I will take the loud one and the other two ahead of us, can you manage the others without tripping over yourself?"

"Do not insult me, girl! I am more than capable of handling these ruffians without your help at all."

"I just would not like to see you exhaust yourself attempting to move all that weight about. If I must contend with them all I would greatly prefer knowing in advance."

"And I do not wish to be troubled by the weakness of your sex. Do not let me turn around and see you on your back with that lice-infested whoreson between your legs!"

"My sex? What do you know of anyone's sex, eunuch? You have not been a man since before you took your vows."

"Lying, blasphemous harpy! I will bless these men myself for taking you off my hands if you do not still your tongue!"

"And I would leave you to them if I could even fathom what use they could have for a fat friar who cannot even get himself up from the ground after his own prayers."

"Enough!" Their assailant's voice cut through the wood like a thunderclap. "I have heard more than my ears can bear, just kill them both and be done with it! Now!"

Elsabeth was on the move before there was even a flicker of motion from their opponents. She lunged to her right and whipped her sword around in a falling cut at the nearest outlaw, while Hieronymus moved to contend with the men behind them. The harsh ring of steel broke the peace of the grove as her blade struck the shaft of her opponent's axe, and she felt the shock of the impact in her hands. The ruffian hooked her sword blade down, but Elsabeth lunged quickly to her left, and raked her sword along the top of his thigh. The blow sheared through muscle and tendon, and she took advantage as his leg collapsed beneath him to wheel her sword around in a high cut that clove off the top of his head. She stepped past his falling corpse, sprung to the right, and twitched her sword into a hanging guard to cover herself from the leader's kriegsmesser as it whistled toward her left shoulder. Steel rang against steel as they exchanged a flurry of blows. Every step Elsabeth took was a little bit further to the right, to keep her third opponent from bringing his cudgel to bear against her.

Her opponent proved quite skilled in managing his weapon, but she immediately noticed his preferences for the flourishes of a tournament fighter. Elsabeth bore into him; every movement short, precise, and simple. The speed of her attacks and counters wore him down, and the showmanship that impressed the crowds on the tournament field soon worked against him. He wheeled his messer around in a blow to her left shoulder. She met his attack with an overhand cut of her own, and as their blades met, she flipped her sword into a short rising cut that sliced the undersides of his wrists. He cried out and lost his hold on his weapon, and Elsabeth quickly reversed her strike into a cut back down into his right shoulder.

She quickly surveyed the scene around her as he fell. The first of Hieronymus's opponents lay still in a spreading pool of blood. Her companion now turned his attention to finishing the other, his staff abandoned in favor of the buckler hung at his belt. Her remaining opponent took note of his leader dying at Elsabeth's feet, then dropped his cudgel and ran. The thud of steel tearing through flesh filled the hall beneath the verdant ceiling of the wood, and Elsabeth turned to find Hieronymus withdrawing his sword from the chest of the last of the ruffians.

For a moment the din of the fight echoed in the grove, then died away. Elsabeth's arms burned with the effort of the fight and her stomach churned from the rush of battle. She mopped the sweat beading on her brow with the back of her hand, and wiped the blood from her sword on the garments of one of their fallen adversaries. Then she looked to Hieronymus.

"Weakness of my sex?" she asked, as she slid her sword into its scabbard with irritation.

"What have you to complain about? It worked, did it not?" he said. "The churl was so irritated by the time he finally got around to ordering his lackeys to kill us, we caught them unprepared."

Elsabeth rolled her eyes and nudged one of the fallen men with her boot. "Just remember that I still owe you a thrashing for getting me into this in the first place once we reach town."

Hieronymus chuckled as he hung his buckler from his belt once more, sheathed his sword, and reclaimed his staff from where he discarded it. He reverently wiped the soil and detritus of the forest floor from it before starting off again down the road. "Would a drink suffice to placate your wrath, my child? There will be plenty to go around tonight."

She twitched one corner of her mouth into a smirk. "Well, that would be a start at least. This trip would be worth it just to see you pay for once."

Chapter II

Travelers making their way along the road between Leyen and Ortenau filled the common room of the inn of Friuli to nearly overflowing that night. They joined with the men of town in drinking and gambling the night away. The roar of their voices and laughter boomed among the wooden beams and plastered walls, and shook the whole of the inn while musicians played a jaunty dance tune in a corner. Oil lanterns hung from the great oak columns filled the room with golden light, and windows along the outside walls let in silver moonlight from the courtyard outside. Women and girls in common dress threaded their way through the patrons to deliver platters of food and tankards of ale, and slipped just beyond the reach of men seeking to pull them into a dance or kiss. The rich fragrance of herbs and cooking food lent the common room an earthy air. Merriment was the rule of the evening, and Elsabeth and Hieronymus dove into the frivolity with zeal.

The friar sat at a table near a corner with a tankard of ale in one hand, and the other around the waist of a woman of the town. His voice carried above the din of the other patrons as he regaled any who would listen with the details of their fight in the woods (with his own part greatly embellished). His antics ensured him an eager audience as he alternately took great pulls from his ale and molested the woman at his side, to the roar of approval from the men around him. Elsabeth plunged into the merrymaking with glee. Her hair rippled freely behind her like a copper banner as she passed from one waiting lap to another, and drank her fill from both her own tankard and those of the men gathered in the common room. She danced with them and added to her share of Hieronymus's haul at the gambling tables. Then approaching the musicians, she shared a deep kiss with one, before turning her affections to another, and soon drew the attention of those gathered away from the serving girls.

The revelry continued late into the night, and as time passed the common room emptied as the townsfolk left to return to their homes and the travelers staggered up to their rooms. Elsabeth was left alone with one of the musicians as the others packed up and headed for their beds. She sat in his lap, now plucking at a lute under his direction, and giggled from time to time when his hands wandered from hers as he guided them along the strings of the instrument to rest on the inside of her thigh or on her bosom. She soon tired of plucking only the lute, and took his hand as she started for the stairs leading to the private rooms above. Hieronymus remained at the table draining the last of the ale from his tankard, and then thumped it down to join the mountain of empty ones stacked at his side. Elsabeth paused.

"You were right," she said. "The pay was quite worth the hassle." Elsabeth swayed a little, and her new friend caught her before she could fall, and pulled her against him.

The friar gave her a self-satisfied smirk. "As I told you, Tetty, nothing to fear at all. Now, if you will pardon me, the lovely lass here has requested that I bring the bishop around for an audience at her nunnery."

Elsabeth chuckled. Her companion nuzzled the back of her neck impatiently and elicited a squeal as one of his hands slipped to the inside of her thigh. She jabbed her elbow into him playfully in response. "Go on, wait for me upstairs!" she said, and then turned her attention back to Hieronymus once the musician had departed after a quick kiss of her hand. "Can you make it on your own, or should I summon a litter for you?"

Hieronymus grunted indignantly and levered himself to his feet with effort. "You need not worry about me, my love. It shall not be me upon my knees for these ministrations."

"Your devotion to your faith is an inspiration to us all, Brother." She sketched a mocking bow.

The friar barked a short laugh before bowing to her awkwardly. The woman in his company seized his soiled robes to ensure he did not collapse on the floor. "Good night, my child, and may the Lord bless and watch over you."

Hieronymus made the sign of the Wheel to her and shuffled out of the inn with the woman supporting him. Elsabeth waited for him to go before turning toward the stairs leading up to the private rooms. She swayed on her feet as she crossed the floor, and nearly ran straight into a cloaked and hooded figure who suddenly loomed up in her path. A gloved hand shot out to catch her wrist when she began to fall and steadied her on her feet again. Elsabeth struggled for a moment against his iron grip.

"Hey! Take your hands off me!" she snapped, and aimed an unsteady blow at him. In her inebriated state she swung wide and nearly fell again.

The Hooded Man easily ducked back from her strike, and his hand on her wrist kept her on her feet. His features were lost in the shadow of his deep woolen cowl, and she could see only a hint of the thick beard covering his chin. "Easy, girl," he said in a low, gravelly voice. "I am not seeking you for my amusement."

Elsabeth threw his hand off as she steadied herself. "What? Why not... I mean, good! Touch me like that again, and the only satisfaction you will know is my sword. If I could remember where I put it last..."

He ignored her threat. "I come with a message: You and the friar just turned over something to Father Garnerius of the Abbey."

She scowled at him. "Our business arrangement with the Abbot is none of your concern."

"On the contrary," he said. "It would be most wise if it did not remain in his possession."

"Then you are welcome to address your concerns with him directly. We were hired to recover it, and we did. The job is done, as am I with you. I have no desire to stand here and conspire with mysterious cloaked figures in the middle of a tavern at night, as that is far too much like some awful minstrel's fancy for my taste. Now if you will excuse me, I have had a long day and am rather in need of a release with the charming gentleman awaiting me in my room."

The Hooded Man sketched a mocking bow. "Then I shall keep you no longer, my lady. I warned you fairly, and whatever danger befalls you is on your own head."

With that, he turned and strode from the inn with the swirl of his cloak. Elsabeth watched him go before turning for the stairs and following after the lutist.

The creak of the floorboards was her only warning. Elsabeth dozed naked in her bedmate's arms beneath her blankets. The moon was just beginning to slip beneath the horizon in the west, and only a faint shaft of weakening silver light spearing through the window illuminated her room. Her head was still heavy with drink, and she nearly missed the sound. Only the shifting of her companion in bed roused her enough to be aware of it.

She remained still. Elsabeth peered into the darkness out of the corner of her eye, and in the faint light she just made out a hunched figure drawing nearer to the bed. A gleam of white briefly flared in his hand as the moonlight caught the blade of the knife he held in a fighting grip.

With no weapon at hand, Elsabeth tensed and seized the covers, and as he drew within a springing step of her, she vaulted from bed and threw them over his head to entangle him in the blanket and slow his attack. Elsabeth took advantage of the distraction while he struggled to free himself, and slammed into him low around his middle, driving him to the floor. Her opponent tried to stab her blindly through the blanket but missed, and when that failed he attempted to overwhelm her with his strength. When her advantage of leverage foiled him he tried to cut his way out instead, and she seized the knife when it slashed through the blanket. With a quick twist of her wrist she wrenched it from his hand, and plunged it down into the struggling intruder. He grunted sickeningly as the blade pierced his belly, and she withdrew her arm and pulled the covers off him as he writhed on the floor, then finished him with a slash across the throat.

She collapsed backward on her rear for a moment to regain her breath. By now her lover was fully awake from the disturbance, but she ignored his cry of alarm at the man dying on the floor and the blood splattered across her naked body. Elsabeth quickly searched the assassin and found a folded slip of parchment tucked away in the pouch at his belt, along with a leather drawstring purse containing a few silver coins. She ignored the inquiries of her companion as she hastily dressed, retrieving her belongings and sword from a wardrobe in one corner of the room. Her doublet rattled slightly as the small metal scales concealed between its linen lining and velvet outer shell moved against each other. Elsabeth tied her assailant's purse to her belt and stuffed the note into a pouch, then hurriedly gathered up her belongings and crammed them into her pack.

The musician seized her by the shoulders when she brushed past in her haste to depart. "Elsie, love, will you stop and tell me what is going on?"

Elsabeth leaned in and kissed him fully on the mouth before pulling away and continuing her preparations. "I am rather sorry to be running out so suddenly, but when someone comes for me with a weapon, I prefer not to wait for his friends. You may wish to leave yourself. I think it will be unwise for you to wait around."

"Where do we meet again?"

"We do not. Take care of those hands of yours," she said. Then she threaded her arms through her jacket, slipped her pack over her shoulder, grabbed her sword, and was out the door before he could respond.

Every shadow stretching out into the darkened streets of Friuli held unseen enemies watching her as Elsabeth rushed through the town. Wood-framed buildings frowned on her with their darkened windows gazing down like empty black eyes. Their fronts crowded the dirt streets, while black alleys stretched back in between them. A few torches sputtered along the walls of the town, but she had only her own night vision to guide her through the winding maze between the inn at the main gate and the brothels in the rundown southern quarter of Friuli. The rush of her fight quickly snapped her drink-addled mind back to clarity, and she cursed at herself for ignoring the warnings of the Hooded Man.

The message she found on the body of her assailant was short and concise:

> *Brother Hieronymus has served his purpose. He travels now with a woman of immoral character. I know not how much they truly know of this business, but consider this purse of twenty silvers an advance on having them removed as a liability. I will double it upon proof your task is completed.*

There was no signature, but the letter was marked with the sign of the Wheel crowned with a tasseled galero. As the words blazed in her mind, she prayed she was not too late for Hieronymus.

The south quarter of Friuli was little more than a collection of hastily constructed, simple wooden shacks crowding around each other within the town's outer brick wall. Narrow and ill-lit streets wound between blocks of buildings thrown up with no regard for planning, and made navigating a confusing maze of alleys and dead end streets cluttered with refuse and hovels. During daylight hours a few stalls offered goods more affordable to the destitute residents of the quarter than those of the market near the main gates, but after sunset the chief commodity was sin.

Finding which establishment Hieronymus chose to patronize took little time; the drunken friar (that was to say, one who gave no thought to concealing his business there) stood out from the normal clientele. The two-story building was one of the south quarter's more ostentatious ones, with brightly painted wooden framing and timber-clad walls, and glazed windows lit from within by the golden glow of lanterns. Two rough-looking men guarding the entrance leered as she approached and looked disdainfully at the sword hung at her hip, but let her pass without hassle. The interior was no less gaudy than the exterior, with painted walls and furnishings, and the overwhelming scent of perfume hanging thickly in the air. An open common room greeted her as she entered, and the establishment did its best to take on the appearance of any normal tavern. Stairs on her right led up to the lodgings on the second floor, and a door opposite the main entrance disappeared into the darkened kitchens. The trestle tables lining the walls were empty at this hour, and all the patrons were now continuing their business in the private rooms upstairs. Almost as she entered, a woman screamed on the floor above, and Elsabeth sprung into motion.

Her sword cleared its scabbard with the rasp of steel on wood and leather, and she charged up the stairs and turned a corner as they reversed back on themselves. A cloaked figure stood on a landing on the second floor, and spun around to meet her as she reached the turn in the stairs. He held a knife in his hand and rushed into her to close the distance before she could bring her sword to bear against him, then struck at her with a level thrust. Elsabeth stepped to her left and pressed her back against the wall, slapped his wrist away with the flat of her sword to pass his knife harmlessly past her, then seized him roughly by the shirt and threw him down the stairs. The assassin cried out as she unbalanced him, and he tumbled down to the floor below in a tangled ball of limbs. He struck the landing with a sickening crunch, and lay there unmoving.

Elsabeth immediately spun and continued the rest of the way up. The commotion drew the attention of the women working the house and their clients, and people in various states of undress emerged from the rooms. The sight of her bared sword sent most of them fleeing back into their chambers, while others rushed down the stairs to see to the fallen man. Elsabeth pushed past them, and spotted the woman Hieronymus left with earlier peering out from one door at the end of the hall. The woman panicked as Elsabeth started for her and tried to close the door, but she struck it hard with her shoulder and forced her way into the room only to find the friar lying naked and unconscious on the floor, with his robes and other belongings discarded around him.

"God!" she said, and dropped her sword with a sharp metallic clatter and knelt beside him. "Hieronymus?" Elsabeth shook him by the shoulder, and her heart leapt into her throat when he did not respond. A bit of drool frothed around his mouth and he continued to lay with his eyes slightly closed. "Hieronymus!"

The friar snorted and began to snore, and Elsabeth let out a relieved sigh.

She looked up at the woman, who shrunk back against a corner opposite the door after Elsabeth broke into the room. "What happened?" she demanded.

The woman shook at the sharpness in her voice. "Nothing, my lady, I swear! He came up here, undressed, and fell asleep right where he was standing!"

Elsabeth sighed and rolled her eyes. "Well, good to know he is himself." She picked up her sword and returned it to its scabbard, then crossed the room to a dresser where a bouquet of flowers in a vase was set out. She discarded the flowers and dumped the water over the dozing friar's head. He snarled a stream of curses in protest as the shock of cold and wet roused him from sleep.

"Lord damn you to torment when I get my hands on whomever you are!" he snapped as he tried to shield his face. Hieronymus panted heavily as he forced himself upright. "What in the name of the Dark One am I doing down here on the floor?"

"You fell asleep, you drunken letch," Elsabeth said. "Get up, we have trouble."

"Elsabeth? What are you doing here? Finally came to your senses about me, eh?"

She smirked. "Only in your prayers, love. I have seen rather more of your orb and scepter just now than I would ever like to again in my life."

Hieronymus tried to stand, but sunk back to the floor with a groan when his drink and sleep-addled limbs refused to cooperate. "Help an old man to his feet, will you, love?" Elsabeth rolled her eyes and took hold of his hand as he tried again. With an effort, and Elsabeth straining on his arm, the friar managed to lever himself back to his feet. He clasped his hands on his prodigious belly. "You should show some respect, my child. The Lord of All has made this body a temple. It is a thing of beauty."

She chuckled and went about retrieving his garments. "In that case he may wish to execute his architect. Get dressed and quickly, we need to get out of here."

He groaned. "What? Why? I have not done a thing."

Elsabeth handed him his clothing, and he took his time to dress again. "I will explain later, but your night is not the only one to be spoiled. You are just lucky I got here when I did, or else you would never have woken again."

"All right, all right," he said. "And where are we going, then?"

"Like I said, I will explain shortly. I would rather not say it here," she said, and eyed the woman watching them nervously from the corner.

"Fine, fine, Tetty. You certainly know how to ruin an old man's night."

Chapter III

Elsabeth and Hieronymus made their way along the darkened streets of Friuli. The friar huffed at her pace, and she wove through several alleyways and cross-streets to lose anyone who might try to follow them from the brothel. She only stopped when they finally emerged from the southern quarter and stood at the base of Abbey Hill, which occupied the entirety of the northern quarter, and straddled the main line of the wall encircling the town. The base of the hill itself was beyond another wall of equal height, which intersected the main fortifications, creating a bulge on the northern end of Friuli. A turret guarded each juncture between the hill and main walls. The Abbey itself looked down from its complex behind a second wall of brick at the hill's summit.

The two pulled up just short of the wall and took shelter in an alley across from the gate. Hieronymus leaned on his staff and glared up at her.

"Well girl, would you mind explaining what all of this is about, and why we are sneaking around like a couple of common thieves?"

Elsabeth reached into her belt pouch, pulled out the note she recovered from her would-be assassin, and handed it to him. "I was attacked as well. And right before I went up to bed, some strange fellow in a hood and cloak stopped me and warned me that we should not let the Abbot have that reliquary we recovered for him."

Hieronymus puzzled over the parchment and frowned. "You think the Abbot sent those men to kill us?"

Elsabeth shrugged. "Either that, or someone sent them in his name. Regardless, I am starting to think there is more to this than just recovering stolen church property."

The friar grunted and handed her back the message. "And here I thought it would be an easy bit of coin."

She smirked. "Easy is not quite as fun. What do you think? Would he have returned it to the high altar?"

"I am not sure. But I would be surprised if the guard has not been increased since the theft."

Elsabeth nodded her agreement. "And if the Abbot is at home, we cannot just walk in ourselves. We need another way in."

"Well," the friar said, "I can think of one way, though it will likely not be a pleasant one."

Elsabeth wrinkled her nose against the stench as she climbed the brick shaft leading up into the Abbey from the sewer tunnels running beneath the hill. She was wedged into its narrow confines — just a little over half again the breadth of her shoulders — with her back against one wall, and her feet jammed into the one across from her. She slowly shimmied upwards in this manner, while Hieronymus waited below.

Above, she could just make out the distant circle that was her only light, and any view of the torch held by her companion below was blocked by her own body. Elsabeth steadily climbed higher. Her legs ached from the effort of driving herself upwards, her shoulders burned from the strain of supporting her weight, and every breath filled her nostrils with the stench of human waste. *Fresh air. Just think of the lovely fresh air when you get the bloody hell out of this hole.*

Long minutes of climbing passed before she finally reached the end of the shaft. The opening at the top was a small round hole, just large enough for her hips to pass through the cut in the wooden planks. She tensed and strained her ears, listening for any sound of someone in the chamber beyond, but heard nothing aside from the gurgle of water in the drainage tunnels far below. With great care, Elsabeth released the straps buckling her sword's scabbard to its baldric and passed it up through the portal overhead. Then she reached through with first one arm, and then the other, and levered herself up. Her head surfaced and she gasped in a draught of fresher air from the Abbot's privy.

Elsabeth strained and pulled herself out of the shaft, wriggling a bit to clear the swelling of her hips and backside, and for a moment sat on the lip of the bench to catch her breath. She retrieved her sword and hung it from her baldric once more, then slowly crept to the door and listened. Silence greeted her once again, so Elsabeth carefully took hold of the handle, pulled it open a crack, and peered through into the darkness beyond.

She could see little in the Abbot's chamber in the darkness of predawn. It was located along the east range of the complex on the second floor of the chapter house, so not even the fading light of the moon found its way in to illuminate it. Elsabeth waited until her eyes adjusted as best she could hope for, and slowly the darkness resolved itself into the dark shadow of a four-post bed in the middle of the room, and other furnishings along the walls. An extensive wardrobe occupied much of the northern wall of the chamber, with a large desk and ornate chair opposite it. A round table and four chairs stood in another corner, where the Abbot could take his meals in private, and a large trunk sat pushed up against the foot of the bed. The floors were bare wood, but a plush rug lay beneath the bed. Of the Abbot himself, she could see no sign.

Elsabeth slunk around the door of the reredorter and slipped the rest of the way into the chamber. A quick search of the wardrobe and desk turned up nothing more than the Abbot's expansive collection of clothes, a few trinkets of his office, letters, and other mundane documents. The trunk was unlocked and held only spare robes and other garments. She swept her eyes across the room but noticed nothing else unusual, until they fixed on a bunched corner of the rug. Elsabeth stepped up and flipped the edge back with the toe of her boot, and revealed a small trapdoor secured with a lock.

She reached into the pouch at her belt and withdrew a folded leather toolkit containing a small hook-shaped pick and torsion wrench. Elsabeth started work on the lock, and it took her little time before the compartment was open. She reached within and removed a tubular object wrapped in fabric the length of her forearm, and the diameter of both her fists. Upon removing the wrappings, she smiled in recognition at the engraved golden form of the reliquary, then quickly covered it again and tucked it under her arm. Elsabeth closed the compartment and covered it with the rug, before retracing her steps back into the reredorter.

As she returned to the privy bench, Elsabeth set her sword down and stuffed the reliquary into her pouch as best she could, then worked herself back through the hole and into the shaft once more. She reached up and pulled her sword down after her before awkwardly making her way down again. This quickly proved more difficult than her ascent, and several times she nearly lost her grip and fell. Her progress slowed significantly as the stench of sewage and waste quickly became unbearable. Her lungs burned for want of clean air, and her shoulders and legs were afire from the effort of descending the length of the shaft. She was perhaps a good story from reaching the bottom when her hold on the sides of the shaft slipped, and she slid the rest of the way down with a shout of alarm.

Elsabeth struck the floor of the sewage tunnel hard on her side, and landed with a splash in a slow river churning with foul water and human waste. She strangled a cry of disgust as she regained her feet and checked herself for any sign of injury. Hieronymus was nowhere in sight with their torch, so she carefully felt her way along the darkened tunnels back toward the dim light of predawn at the tunnel entrance. She emerged from the drainage gate and limped off to a dark corner nearby, where she found Hieronymus dozing propped against the wall. She prodded him roughly with her toe and he awakened with a start.

"God damn you, Tetty!" he snapped when he fully awoke. "I would have thought you of all people would have learned by now how to properly wake a man."

Elsabeth scowled down at him. "Even if I had the desire to, we would not have time, love. I have it. We should probably make ourselves hard to find."

Hieronymus levered himself back to his feet with the support of his staff and wrinkled his nose in disgust. "God in heaven, what is that smell? You should consider a bath."

"I have been knee deep in the blessed shit of the Abbot, which I hope is good enough to wash away at least a few of my sins. And next time, you can climb the privy shaft if you would not plug it first."

"I am a brother of the Wheel, child, I do not wallow in excrement."

"No, just your ale and whores."

They started off down the street at a hurried pace, but did not get far before the shadowed figure of a man appeared in front of them. Elsabeth's hand went to her sword hilt, but three other figures closed in suddenly around them, and she saw the faint glint of metal in their hands as knives were drawn. A familiar voice broke the silence of Friuli's darkened streets.

"Well," the Hooded Man said, "I see you finally decided to heed my warning."

Elsabeth released her sword and scowled. "You would be amazed at how effectively having someone trying to stab you in your sleep can make you consider it."

The man chuckled, a low, throaty sound. "Indeed. I am pleased to see you had not abandoned all of your wits over drink and a little romp with wandering minstrels. Just the one, or did you have your way with them all?"

She scowled. "My sleeping habits are none of your concern. What do you want?"

"The reliquary. I assume that you decided to retrieve it?"

Hieronymus glared. "Listen here, my son, I know not what this matter is about, but if you intend to make accusations against a fellow man of the Wheel, I think I am entitled to hear it."

"In time, Brother," the Hooded Man said. "And then you can go back to your wenching and drinking, which I am sure his Grace the Prince-Bishop finds quite becoming of one of his brothers. Now. The reliquary."

He extended his hand and the armed men around them closed in threateningly. They were too close for her to draw her sword, and they left her with no room to maneuver if it came to blows. She sighed and retrieved the reliquary from her pouch, and handed it over. The Hooded Man discarded the cloth wrapping, and she and Hieronymus both gasped: She had flattened the reliquary beneath her in her fall, and a veneer of gold plating flaked away in places, to expose the thin lead making up the bulk of the tube.

"A fake!" Elsabeth said in surprise.

The Hooded Man nodded. "Had it not been for you two fools killing the men I sent to retrieve it in the first place, this would be well on its way to the Bishop by now. I did not count on Father Garnerius noticing it missing so quickly." He easily tore the soft lead sheet of the reliquary apart, and removed several pieces of rolled parchment concealed within.

"What is that?" she asked.

"Deeds and titles, pretty. Father Garnerius has been buying, or extorting, property from some of the lesser landholders around Friuli for some purpose. The Bishop has heard rumors of this, and would like to know why." He held one of the pieces of parchment close to his face to better study it in the dim light. "Interesting... Lord Cuncz."

Elsabeth frowned. "Cuncz?"

"The Baron of Leyen, pretty. It seems that most of this land was acquired by the Abbot on the Baron's behalf." He quickly folded up the papers and stuffed them into his pouch. "The Bishop will be most pleased, but I believe in being thorough." The darkness of predawn, and the shadow of his hood, masked the man's features, but Elsabeth felt him regarding her and Hieronymus carefully. "You two seem to have no trouble taking coin for a good deed, perhaps you can be convinced to take his Grace's coin as well?"

Elsabeth folded her arms across her chest. "What do you have in mind?"

"If Father Garnerius is acquiring this land on Lord Cuncz's behalf, quite likely Cuncz himself may have certain...incriminating information in his possession the Bishop may greatly desire to see. I would like you to retrieve it for me. And I can promise you will be much better rewarded than with a knife in the dark."

Chapter IV

The town of Leyen stood on the south bank of a river, two days' walk east of Friuli and on the point bar of a bend in the watercourse as it meandered southwesterly across the plain. The land on both sides, owned by Lord Cuncz, was rich and fertile, and cultivated farmland stretched for miles in all directions. A wall of brick encircled the town upon a slight rise, and a channel cut across the meander enclosed it within a moat that was spanned by gated bridges on three sides. The city was a maze of cobbled streets threading between clustered blocks of homes, markets, and workshops. Inns crowded near each of the town's gates, and a cathedral, with vaulted arches and expansive windows of colored glass, dominated the town square.

Cuncz's castle and residence, a fortified manor on a lawn of green grass, stood beyond a series of walls on the north end of Leyen. The estate intersected the town's main fortifications, in a manner much akin to Friuli's, with turrets spaced at regular intervals around it. Another channel, cut from the river, passed through the town wall on either side of the castle via tunnels sealed with iron grates to form a moat around the inner wall. It was spanned by a drawbridge which was accessed by a white cobbled path lined with trees leading up from the town. The pathway continued through the well-fortified gatehouse, and by the gardens and ornamental fish pools that filled the bailey within the manor walls.

They arrived in the waning hours of the day, and the town was still alive with the calls of merchants, beggars, and the steady drone of foot and cart traffic along the narrow winding streets. Elsabeth and Hieronymus set themselves up in an inn near the west gate. Their chosen residence was more opulent than the rustic taverns of Friuli, but their arrival passed without fanfare and only a cursory interest as they settled in.

She sat now at a table in the crowded common room, dressed in a fine cotehardie of deep red linen, with her hair braided under an organza veil. Beside her sat Hieronymus, in a green brocade doublet and woolen hose in the fashion of a merchant. His garments strained to contain his bulk and fit him closely, displaying rather more of him than Elsabeth found pleasant.

Three other men of middle age, dressed in similar fashion, shared their table with them as they took their evening meal. Elsabeth watched them closely and flashed demure smiles whenever it seemed Hieronymus was not paying attention to her, while he conversed with them over the day's news. Evening passed into night, and the five now sat quietly; the four men nursing tankards of ale, while around them the patrons of the common room began to disperse to their own rooms or homes.

"Thank you again for sharing your table with my daughter and me this evening," Hieronymus said. "It is so crowded I feared we would be confined to our room!"

"You chose a rough time to visit Leyen, friend," said one of the men. He had a lean face, dark blue eyes, and neat blonde beard, with hair to his shoulders. He called himself Jacobus. "Midsummer is the busiest time for trade in the town."

Hieronymus nodded and raised a finger pointedly. "Perhaps, but I imagine it is the most lucrative."

Another of their new companions, Clement, who was clean-shaven and green-eyed, with brown hair cropped short, chuckled into his tankard of ale. Elsabeth flashed him a coy smile and the traveler smiled back, leaning in slightly to ingratiate himself with their guests. "Indeed it is. Fortunately, there are a few good places left to put up a stall in the market. You will want to start your day rather early to make sure to claim one, however."

"This is, of course, our first visit to this town; I pray I do not hope too much that you gentlemen would be so kind as to offer your guidance, seeing as you are more familiar with the lay of the land, eh?"

Elsabeth glanced shyly at the third. His face was broad and plain, with a thick brown mustache and beard, shoulder-length brown hair and piercing blue eyes. He introduced himself as Thadeus and he nodded eagerly, "It would be my pleasure to help a fellow traveler find his way about."

"Then I would be greatly indebted to you, my friend. Tell me, this is a safe town, yes? I would hate for my daughter to be set upon by some manner of ruffian when she takes her air, or for my goods to be pillaged from under me."

Jacobus leaned back in his chair and swirled his tankard thoughtfully. Elsabeth watched him carefully from the corner of her eye for the slightest hint of deceit or hesitance. "The Baron certainly keeps the peace. I have heard scarce word of trouble with such lawless men within the walls of Leyen."

Hieronymus leaned in and took all three men in with a solemn glance, and continued with lowered voice. "Tell me, what manner of man is he? It is frightfully difficult upon the road for men such as we. And sad to say that, in these days, there is often little means to tell the difference between the barons and the local highwaymen. Road taxes, escort taxes, inspections. Many are the days I felt that there is less profit in trade than in taking up arms and joining the ruffians preying on the roads myself." He made a show of taking Elsabeth's hand and stroking it. She quickly and quietly kicked his shin under the table in response, but he ignored her. "If it were not for my dear child, of course. I could never subject her to such a life, or men of such distasteful disposition. Better to send her off to a convent than to think of her dallying with such rabble."

"I must confess we see little of Lord Cuncz," Thadeus said. "He spends much of his time in solitude within the castle, and I cannot recall having seen him set foot beyond its walls in any visit I have made here. Though I have heard he at times can be seen walking the outer walls during the morning hours."

"No one to my knowledge has ever received an audience with him either," said Clement. "All matters between the town and castle are handled by the Chamberlain or the Captain of the Guard."

"You must have wax in your ears." Jacobus scoffed. "I have overheard some of the gate guards say that at times during his morning walks he spies a young lass in the gardens along the moat that takes his fancy, and has her brought to the castle for the night. Then there are the stories of a sealed carriage arriving late at night that is taken all the way to the castle. No one seems to know who the passenger is, but it always leaves again before dawn."

Hieronymus chuckled and took a swig from his tankard. "Even I could take a guess at that. It is probably nothing more mysterious than some other mistress paying a visit. Perhaps the wife or daughter of the neighboring lord he wishes to keep fewer tongues from wagging over than a common girl of the town."

"I wonder who that might be, then, as Lord Emrich who is the nearest has no official issue. Of course, there is Friuli as well, but the good Father has no...nieces of his own."

Clement chuckled into his ale. "Then I suspect Father Garnerius is the only resident of the Abbey with no such near kin. There seems to be a plague of men of the Wheel, left to care for unfortunate nieces and nephews of mysterious pedigree. Still, I suspect our friend here is correct, that Lord Cuncz has found some lady he fancies. And good thing, too, for Leyen still harbors uneasy memories of Lord Rupertus."

Elsabeth quirked an eyebrow. "Lord Rupertus?" she asked. The three men looked her way at her unexpected intonation, for she spoke little as her part in their masquerade, and all three showed great eagerness to respond to her.

Thadeus found his voice first and leaned in conspiratorially. "Lord Cuncz's father," he said in a hushed voice, "And yet not. Lord Rupertus's wife died in childbirth many years ago, and the child she bore perished with her. Lord Rupertus was devastated by this, and never took another bride, nor even showed interest in another woman for the rest of his life. But this also left him with a problem as his age advanced, for with no issue and near kin, what would become of Leyen when he passed?"

Clement broke in to take up the tale before the other could finish. "Some years ago, however, he accepted a youth into his household, and adopted and legitimized him. Thus Lord Cuncz assumed the title of Baron when Lord Rupertus died."

"And whence did the youth come?" Hieronymus asked.

Jacobus shrugged. "No one rightly knows. He merely appeared one day at Lord Rupertus's side." He finished his tankard with one last draught. "There is sadly little else to say of the matter, as Lord Cuncz guards his privacy closely, and even his subjects scarcely know him. Now if you will excuse me, the hour grows late and I wish an early start setting out my wares on the morrow. Good evening to you all."

He pushed himself away from the table and bowed politely at the waist. His eyes lingered on hers for a moment, and Elsabeth coyly glanced away with a tight-lipped smile for his benefit. Then he turned and strode from the common room. Their remaining companions grudgingly acknowledged the deepening night and begged their leave as well. Elsabeth offered each a shy smile in the manner of the first, and they too, departed to their private rooms, each certain that they alone shared an unspoken promise with the merchant's demure daughter.

Hieronymus levered himself to his feet and turned to her. "Well daughter, I think it is time to see to our own rest. If you would be so kind as to help an aging man to his room."

Elsabeth stood as well, and threaded her arm through his as they made their way toward their room. She leaned toward him and spoke with a low voice. "I think you are rather overplaying it."

"Nonsense, Tetty. And you are certainly one to talk. I have seen strumpets in a nunnery act with greater subtlety. No daughter of mine should be seen batting her eyes about a tavern like a common whore."

"Watch who you call common! Besides, it got us a meal without having to dip into our own purses, and kept them more focused on me than the questions you were asking. Better to send them off to their beds with lustful dreams, than for them to remember a pair of strangers prying about Lord Cuncz."

Hieronymus grunted. "Well, then perhaps you should make your rounds to give them something to really remember. That should ensure all they have to recall is the charms the Lord of All has blessed you with. And when you are finished, your dear father could certainly do with some company for the rest of the night."

Elsabeth rolled her eyes. "When you say it in such a way I can hardly imagine why I have refused your bed for so long. Regretfully

I must decline. After all, you have an early start tomorrow to provide for us, and I must make arrangements to meet with Lord Cuncz."

They reached their private room, and Elsabeth opened the door. She playfully shoved Hieronymus through before following after and closing it behind him. The friar stumbled forward and caught himself with a curse, followed by rapidly making the sign of the Wheel. "And how do you intend to do such a thing, if no one is ever admitted to the castle?

Elsabeth smirked at him and crossed the room. In one corner stood a full-length mirror, and she made a show of admiring her figure in it. "Oh, I think I may have something in mind."

Chapter V

The next morning dawned bright and clear, and before the sun rose above the eastern span of the town wall, the denizens began their morning routines. Cooking fires in the hearths of homes and the kitchens of the town's inns filled the gloom of pre-dawn with pleasant aromas, and merchants prepared their stalls in the many market squares. Tents and pavilions of brightly painted canvas sprung up like a field of garish flowers in the heart of the main square. Overlooked by the towering edifice of the Cathedral of Leyen, it was the most prestigious of all the markets in Leyen. A rosy blush bloomed on the horizon to the east as the sun appeared, and with it more of the townsfolk awakened and took to the paved streets to see to their morning business.

Elsabeth awoke early and dressed, while Hieronymus snored from the couch that sat along one wall of their room. She slipped a simple gown of rich, green wool over her chemise, then carefully adjusted the lacing that ran from her navel to the square neckline, fitting her dress snugly down to her hips to best flaunt the curve of her figure. Once she felt satisfied by her appearance, she quietly slipped from the room and across the inn. She stepped alone onto the streets of Leyen, just as the sun crested the battlements of the wall to the east.

By now there was considerable activity around the town. A distant buzz of voices filled the air as merchants directed their servants in erecting pavilions and stalls, and laying out their wares for the pedestrians who would soon be crowding the streets. A few carts laden with goods trundled through gates, now opened to the world beyond the town walls. Small numbers of travelers, dressed in fashion both fine and common, mingled on the roads in a display of organized chaos. Exquisitely dressed riders on well-groomed horses made their way along elevated curbs, along with a few people of station who chose to walk. The rest of the foot traffic proceeded on the edge of the street.

Elsabeth stepped out into the traffic and kept to the edges of the road nearest to the raised curbs. She cut a meandering path through the town, and stopped at times at one of the few stands where merchants were already hawking their goods. Anyone who might follow saw only a young woman taking the morning air and browsing the market.

It took her little time to reach the moat that encircled the inner wall around the central keep. The wall itself rose like a sheer cliff of carefully placed bricks from the edge of the water. She judged the moat to be some thirty feet across, with a green lawn stretching from the near bank to a tall hedge hiding it from view from the street. Decorative arches allowed access within, and created a secluded park on either side of the bridge leading into the bailey.

Elsabeth passed through one of the arches. A small number of women gathered within to make use of the moat to do their washing, or to fetch water for the morning cooking. A few trees provided shade, and Elsabeth found a place beneath a willow that was growing on the bank. She slipped her shoes from her feet, drew her skirts up around her knees, and seated herself in the embrace of the gnarled roots stretching down into the water. She let her feet dangle down into the moat, and reclined against the willow's trunk.

The morning was warm and the water was cool against the bare skin of her feet and calves, and she took some time to relax and listen to the growing din as Leyen awoke beyond the hedge.

After some time a lone shadow, silhouetted against the morning sky, detached from the turret flanking the gatehouse, and slowly strolled along the top of the battlement heading in her direction. Elsabeth yawned and stretched, and picked up her shoes before rising to her feet. She could see little of the figure approaching, but could tell he was unarmored and perhaps wore a sword at his hip.

With shoes in one hand and the other holding up her skirts, Elsabeth began to walk along the moat toward the figure on the battlement. As she drew nearer to standing across from him, she found a place where the grass grew all the way down to the water's edge and lowered herself with practiced grace, with her long legs beneath her, and her skirt pulled up just enough to bare her calves. A gentle breeze stirred her finer hairs, which flashed like streams of molten copper in the morning sun. Out of the corner of her eye she saw the shadow atop the battlements stop and lean against the parapet, almost directly across from her. Elsabeth gazed into the water and hooked her hair behind her ear. Though the movement of the water disturbed his reflection, she nonetheless could make out his form, and for several long minutes he stood and watched. She could not tell where he was looking, but before long he called one of the guards to his side and leaned in, as if to whisper for a moment, before he finally resumed his walk, glancing back in her direction at times, before finally disappearing out of sight. She quirked a tight smile, and when he was gone Elsabeth slipped her shoes back on her feet, rose, and began the walk back to the inn.

***

"Have you lost all grasp of your wits, girl?" Hieronymus said.

Elsabeth rolled her eyes as she adjusted the fit of her blue velvet cotehardie. When she relayed her plan to Hieronymus his reaction was much as she anticipated. The knock on their door at the inn by a courier from the Baron, and the perfumed note summoning her to the castle for the evening, did little to calm him. She carefully arranged the square neckline of the dress to bare a generous hint of her cleavage. "Will you stop your complaining? I know what I am doing."

"Oh, I bet you do. I bet you can scarcely contain your excitement at notching your bedpost with a nobleman for a change."

She glared. "It is not like you have room to talk, hypocrite. Or need I remind you about the daughter of the Graf of Ehrenfels?"

"That was not what it looked like! I will have you know my only concern was for the soul of that poor girl." He made the sign of the Wheel as if to lend divine support to his protest, but knowing better, Elsabeth could only bark out a sharp laugh.

"Yes, as I heard it, you started with her sole, then moved up her calves, and then her thighs, before settling in between them. You know that if there is anything incriminating against Lord Cuncz he will likely have it here. That means we needed some way into the castle to look for it. I, for one, would rather it not be up yet another privy shaft. I am merely taking the opportunity that presented itself."

"So instead of climbing up one privy shaft, you decide to invite him up your own. Very clever, Tetty."

Elsabeth retrieved a small velvet bag from her pack, opened the drawstring, and emptied its contents into her palm. A gold pendant, fashioned into the form of a six-spoke Wheel, with the space in between each spoke filled with cloisonné work of red enamel, fell out. She fastened it about her neck on a length of gold chain, and adjusted it so the wheel nestled itself in her cleavage. "I would think you, of all people, would know when a man is at his most vulnerable. Remember that thief in Basel? She made off with half your collections after one night, as I recall. And this would hardly be the first time I have taken advantage of it myself." She thumbed the Wheel hung about her neck. "Besides, I do have this, so I am prepared."

"May the Lord of All have mercy on you for your impertinence, using the Wheel in such a manner."

Elsabeth took a brush from her pack and began working on her hair. Hieronymus glowered at her back with his arms folded across his ample gut. He still wore his merchant's garb, topped now with a ridiculous floppy hat with a feather stuck into the band, from his day feigning work in the markets. She smirked at him in the mirror. "This from the man who I have seen use his staff of office to scratch an inconvenient itch in the most unholy of places?"

"My nethers are none of your concern...

"Now that is a blessing from on high."

Hieronymus shot her a dirty look as he continued. "...and there are better ways than opening yours to a wet-nosed princeling, whom I can tell you I have sown my oats in much fairer fields in the last month than he has in his lifetime. How do you even know this mad scheme of yours will work?"

She pulled her forelocks back from her face and secured them at the back of her head, leaving the rest of her hair to spill freely down her back like a banner of copper. "No more mad than waltzing into a den of brigands to retrieve the reliquary that got us into this bloody mess in the first place." Elsabeth picked up the summons and deftly walked it through her fingers. She stopped, placed the note under her nose and took in the rich fragrance of the perfume. "Clearly I caught the Lord Cuncz's fancy during my walk this morning, and so he summons me to the castle intending to use his charms on the simple merchant's daughter, to entice her into his bed. It will work, of course, but what he does not know is that I am actually taking him in by letting him believe his attempts to woo me are working. I remain in full control of my faculties while I put him in my pocket. He has his bit of fun, and when he finishes and falls asleep, I am free to slip away."

Hieronymus threw up his hands in exasperation. "The King of All needs no rival in the Underworld, for he has woman on earth to contend against him!" He sighed and let his hands fall to his sides in resignation. "Fine, do what you will, but I pray it does not end with me having to bury you after the hanging."

"Just gather up all our things and arrange swift passage away from Leyen. Whether or not I find what we are looking for, I suspect we will need to be away from here with haste. Meet me on the far side of the west bridge at dawn." She flashed him a mischievous smile that did little to assuage the friar's concerned expression. "And as I said: I know what I am doing. Trust me."

Elsabeth finished her preparations while ignoring Hieronymus's fretting. And as the day waned into twilight, an official-looking, mousy little man, dressed in a fine brocaded doublet, arrived flanked by a pair of guards bearing halberds. He greeted her with a graceful bow and said, "Good evening, my lady. I am Conrat, Chamberlain to my Lord Cuncz, Baron of Leyen. I have been commanded to see you safely to his residence," before ushering her off with scarcely a chance to bid farewell to her "father." Hieronymus watched her go with a scowl, and Elsabeth was led from the inn with the guards close around her, leaving no illusion that the invitation she received was merely a polite formality.

The streets of Leyen were still rather crowded, and only slowly did the throngs of pedestrians disperse to the inns or their own homes. A few looked her way as she was escorted through the darkening streets, but otherwise showed little interest at a sight she reasoned they must be accustomed to seeing. As the crowds thinned the sweeps and street-cleaners appeared to scrub away the refuse of the day's activities, and lamp wrights made their rounds to light the town's many street lanterns.

They reached the bridge leading into the castle grounds as full darkness settled over Leyen, and the pale disk of the moon peeked above the battlements to the east. Conrat led her over the drawbridge, and they passed without challenge through the massive gatehouse guarding entry to the outer bailey. A few courtiers of Cuncz's household strolled through the gardens and watched her pass, and the still waters of the fish pools reflected the stars just winking to life in the deepening sky overhead. Barracks, stables, and storerooms crowded against the inside of the outer defenses, while another wall encircling the manor itself loomed up ahead of them. Turrets rose at the northeast and southwest corners of this rampart, both as a last line of defense, and to provide an admirable view of the town and river beyond the outer walls.

Upon passing through a last fortified gate into the inner bailey, they emerged once more in another quiet garden encircled by the inner wall and the buildings within the complex. The manor itself sat backed against the wall in the northwest corner, while guesthouses clustered opposite it to the southeast. All were built of brick, with narrow windows on the lowest two floors, and larger ones gazing out from the upper levels, and peaked and tiled roofs. The manor itself was a large central structure, four stories tall with two short wings of lesser height on either side that each ended in a square tower the height of the central wing. The front entrance was a vaulted arched doorway in the main wing. Golden light shone from the windows and beckoned to those in the gardens as night descended. At the center of the bailey stood a fountain of white stone surrounded by matching benches on a lawn of green grass, and the quiet trickle of water splashing into the basin filled the air. Guards patrolled the inner wall of the bailey and manned the turrets at either corner of the complex. Servants passed between the guest houses, manor, and store rooms, and groundskeepers finished their daily maintenance, and departed for their own quarters and evening meals.

Elsabeth followed Conrat to the main entrance of the manor. A guard stood at either side of the door and opened it as the party approached, allowing them into the antechamber out of dusk's gathering gloom. She found herself in a small, low-ceilinged entry chamber that opened out onto a broader hall with wooden floors and plastered walls. Gilt lanterns illuminated the interior with rich golden light, making the wooden floors and furnishings seem to glow. The Chamberlain directed her forward, past guardrooms on either side of the hall, to another doorway, and ushered her into the great hall itself before he and her escort departed.

As she entered, the low ceiling of the passage from the main entrance gave way to a lofty and expansive chamber some three stories high that occupied almost the entirety of the central wing. Carved wooden columns supported the ceiling high overhead, along with a balcony ringing the second and third levels of the hall. Doors centered in the walls on her left and right led to the east and west wings through carved stone archways. The floor of polished marble tiles, in a variety of colors, formed intricate geometric patterns, and reflected the light of lanterns hung from the timbers supporting the ceiling. A large gilt crown-shaped chandelier, with many candles covered by prisms of glass, was suspended over the center of the floor and provided additional lighting, and with the lanterns lent the hall a golden glow. Large trestle tables stood folded and tucked away in both corners, and atop a dais at the far end of the hall, reached by a flight of five steps, was another long table against the wall. A high-backed chair of ornate gilt wood stood at the center of the dais. The chair was vacant, and a man of about her age stood at the foot of the dais with his hands folded behind his back. Elsabeth's heart fluttered in spite of herself as she first laid her eyes on the Baron of Leyen.

Despite her height, Lord Cuncz's lean and athletic frame matched, if not exceeded, hers and his face she could describe as almost painfully handsome, with a strong jaw and defined features. His keen and intelligent eyes were a piercing blue, and Elsabeth felt as if his gaze could peer clear through her. Though she found his eyes unsettling, his smile was exhilarating. It was broad and lopsided, with one corner of his mouth pulled up as he laid eyes on her when she entered the great hall. It was confident, and superior, and welcoming, but with a slightly predatory edge that lent him a hint of danger. For a moment her breath caught and she maintained her composure only with a great deal of effort, though his searching eyes did not miss the slight catch in her measured pace. Brown hair flecked with gold, worn loosely to his shoulders, framed his face, and he wore a short and neatly-trimmed mustache and a patch of beard on his chin. Though finely groomed, he dressed relatively simply in dark woolen hose that fit him so closely Elsabeth's eyes could not help but stray, and a burgundy brocaded doublet.

Elsabeth reached the foot of the dais, took the skirt of her gown in either hand, and curtsied deeply in such a manner that afforded him a nearly unimpeded view down her dress. As she returned fully to her feet, Cuncz stepped forward and took her hand.

"Welcome to my home," he said in a smooth and cultured voice. "I pray the manner of my summons caused you and your father no alarm, but after I spied you from the battlement this morning, I could not chase the thoughts of you from my mind. Such beauty is a rare sight in Leyen, and I could not bear for it to pass and only see it from afar." Cuncz brought her hand to his lips and gently kissed the back of her fingertips.

Elsabeth blushed fiercely, and her heart skipped at the touch of his hand. *Get hold of yourself, girl, it was not that good! You have heard better than this from stable boys drunk out of their wits!* "My lord flatters me greatly," she said as she shyly turned her head away with embarrassment that was only partially feigned. "Surely in a magnificent city such as this, there are many women of much greater beauty than I, and certainly those of higher standing."

Cuncz's lopsided smile broadened and he stepped closer to her. "Higher standing, perhaps, but certainly not of greater beauty." He threaded his arm through hers and walked her up the dais. At some unspoken command, servants quickly entered from doors concealed at the rear of the hall. They were bearing a small round table and chairs, and placed them atop the dais behind the high seat. "May I ask your name, my dear? I do not wish for us to remain strangers to one another."

"Gwenhevare, my lord," she said.

"Ah, quite lovely, and quite fitting. I must commend you on the skill of your tongue as well, then, for you speak our language quite well. Unless I miss my guess, you are from Coventry?"

Elsabeth swore inwardly. That choice of name led him too near the mark. "I am," she said. "But my father travels widely, and desired I be well-learned in many languages." She favored him with a coy smile and a slight lowering of her chin so she could look up at him through her lashes. "My tutors found my tongue to be quite able to the task."

Cuncz's face colored slightly, but he maintained his composure as he helped her into her seat. From the corner of her eye she caught him stealing a look down the front of her dress, and his hand lingered on hers for just a moment longer than protocol would deem appropriate. Then he released her and rounded the table to his own seat. As if waiting for their Lord to be seated, servants reappeared from the hidden doors. Even from this better vantage, Elsabeth still could see no sign of their hinges or latches. Bearing silver plates and two crystal goblets, they quickly laid out the table. With the plates were a matched set of a knife, spoon and, much to her surprise, a fork. She picked it up and eyed it with wonder. Cuncz noted her reaction and chuckled with amusement.

"It is a new fashion coming out of the Free City-States," he said. "They have been replacing their skewers with actual forks. That is, of course, whence this set came, and they are the first in all of Boehm. Not even the Emperor himself has yet commissioned a set."

Elsabeth blushed in genuine embarrassment, and she suddenly felt very unenlightened and uncouth. "I have never seen such a thing," she said.

Cuncz's lopsided smile broadened. "I insist on staying at the very forefront of fashion, and I suspect they will displace skewers at all the tables soon enough. But we are not here to discuss the finer points of cutlery, though I daresay your father might have an interest. He does deal in silver, does he not?"

The coloring of her cheeks this time was much more intended for Cuncz's benefit. "My lord is quite well-informed."

"In my position I find it quite useful to know what goes on within my walls. I knew of your arrival in Leyen the moment you set foot within the gate, though I nearly punished the guard over the tales he spun of your beauty. Until I saw you for myself from the walls, I thought surely the man was telling mad lies."

Elsabeth smiled shyly and forced a little more color into her cheeks. Before either of them could speak again, the servants returned once more. One filled her goblet with a strong red wine from the City-States, while others carried in three silver platters and two matching silver bowls. One tray was piled high with baked morels wrapped in pastry, upon another, buns of fried cheese and white bread rolled into balls. A third was laden with beetroots marinated in wine, spiced with anise seeds, coriander, and caraway, and layered with horseradish. The servants placed bowls of watercress salad dressed with oil and vinegar for each of them, while the platters were set in the middle of the table where she and Cuncz could select from them as they desired. Once all was placed, they retreated back through the hidden doors, closing out the aroma of spices, herbs, and roasting meat beginning to waft from the kitchens beyond.

Cuncz watched her as he popped a baked morel into his mouth — his lips quirked into that lopsided smile — as if gauging her reaction to the meal's opening course. *Well, he certainly is doing his best to impress me.* She allowed an expression of awed delight to light her features as she surveyed the variety of food presented to her. "I do hope you are hungry," he said, his own expression one of satisfied amusement at her reaction. "I am afraid my cooks had little time to prepare, so the starters might be rather more lacking than I would like, but I pray you find my table to be adequate nonetheless."

Elsabeth reached for her wine and took a drink. As she suspected, it was a potent one, with a hint of apple and oak. *Best be careful with that, or I might be dancing on the table well before dinner is over.* She took just enough wine to leave him the impression of being overwhelmed by the victuals laid out before them, and set the goblet aside. "My lord is modest, I have never seen such a table as this, even on high feast days," she said breathily, then chewed her lip and appraised the marinated beets eagerly. She hesitated a moment with one hand poised to snatch one from the tray, and glanced at him as if she sought his permission to proceed. Cuncz chuckled in amusement and waved for her to continue. Elsabeth took one with feigned excitement and popped it in her mouth. It was strong and spicy, and she made a show of sucking the wine marinade from her fingers with a playful smile. His eyes widened slightly in response and he took a hurried drink from his wine.

A course of: goose stuffed with onions, quinces, pears, and bacon roasted on a spit; applesauce spiced with wine, sugar, cinnamon, saffron, and ginger; and white cabbaged cooked with chicken in spiced beef broth, followed the starter course.

After this came the main course: deer that was first boiled and then simmered in pepper sauce, carrots roasted with beef broth, and cubed parsnips roasted in a mixture of the same broth and butter.

Once they finished with the main course, the servants returned one last time with trays of fruit tartlets, almond and raisin pastries, and a variety of nuts coated with sugar and spiced with nutmeg, ginger, and cloves.

Elsabeth ate her fill and allowed herself to enjoy Cuncz's hospitality. She privately admitted he provided quite an impressive table, even under such short notice. She took great care due to the potency of the wine, imbibing only enough that might be reasonable for a merchant's daughter overwhelmed by an evening of dining far above her station, while still leaving her in control of her faculties. Even with that effort, she nonetheless found her head beginning to swim as the evening wore on, and she fell into occasional giggling fits at the Baron's flirtations. *Focus, girl! Hieronymus will never let you hear the end of it if you pass out before you can do what you came here to do!*

Elsabeth helped herself to another tartlet. "You certainly seem to fancy those," Cuncz said as he watched her over the lip of his goblet, with that same lopsided smile on his face. There was a slight slurring of his speech from the impressive quantity of wine he drank over dinner, and his eyes were half-lidded.

She blushed slightly in genuine embarrassment, as she realized that aside from a handful of the sugared nuts, Cuncz had scarcely touched the desert course and already half the tartlets were gone. Elsabeth flashed him a playful grin and dipped the tip of her little finger into the filling — this one made with cherries — and withdrew it again. She then gave her fingertip a slow lick. "They are wonderful," she said truthfully. "Especially the cherry ones, you should have a taste."

Cuncz's smile became an amused smirk. "I would rather like to, but it seems that you have laid claim to the last of them."

Tartlet still in hand, Elsabeth rose smoothly from her seat and glided with an exaggerated swaying of her hips around the table. When she reached him, she leaned over with a toss of her head to move her hair away from her face, dipped her index finger into the filling, and held it out for him. Cuncz took her finger in his mouth and sucked the filling off, before trying to pull her down into his lap. She giggled playfully and stuffed the tart in his mouth as she retreated out of reach, just far enough to force him out of his chair. He followed after her while quickly finishing the tartlet, caught her by the wrist before she could reach her own chair, and pulled her close, kissing her firmly but gently on the mouth.

Elsabeth allowed him a moment, as if the wine had slowed her recognition of what he intended, then pushed him away with a feigned gasp of shock. "My lord!" she said, hoping her tone sounded sufficiently scandalized to the ears of anyone who might be able to overhear. "This would not be proper of me." She let her cheeks color fiercely and ducked her head away from him shyly.

Cuncz cupped her chin and gently turned her head back to face him. He flashed that lopsided smile again and her heart fluttered in spite of itself. "There is no need to worry, my dear. Not a soul here would breathe a whisper of what might happen tonight."

She made a show of trying to push away, and stumbled awkwardly when she freed herself from his grip. "I really must return, my father worries so," she said, slurring her speech for effect as she swayed uneasily and collapsed toward him. Cuncz darted forward to catch her, as she intended, and pulled her close against his chest. "Oh my..."

He helped her regain her feet, but a hand against the small of her back kept her pressed against him. "I think you may have partaken too liberally of the wine." There was a note of concern in his voice. "It is a touch stronger than I suspect you are accustomed to, I fear. You are in no condition to make it all the way to the inn tonight, and I cannot rest easily with the thought of some misfortune befalling you on the road. I insist you remain here with me tonight and I will see to it that your father has no need to worry for you." He brushed her hair back from her face and stroked her cheek. "I would very much like to share the full extent of my hospitality with you."

His lopsided smile broadened further to hint at the meaning behind his words. Elsabeth hesitated a moment, before allowing a smile of her own to cross her lips. "It would not be proper of me to refuse such a gallant offer."

He leaned in and kissed her again, and this time Elsabeth kissed him back fully, and with a carefully gauged measure of eagerness he returned in kind. She smiled inwardly as his hands caressed her back and one dipped toward her backside. *Hieronymus worries too much, everything is going just as I planned.*

Chapter VI

Things were not, in fact, going as planned.

Elsabeth lay naked in the bed with her eyes closed, at once both attempting to slow her breathing and relax her body to feign sleep, and trying very hard not to actually do just that. She felt Lord Cuncz's lean body pressed up against her back, one arm propping up his head as he watched her, while the other encircled her waist and hugged her close to him. At times the hand about her waist slipped away to gently stroke her shoulder, or glide up her ribcage to fondle her breasts, or slip down her belly and caress the space between her legs. Then he would lift the fall of her copper locks away from the back of her neck, so he could deliver soft kisses to her neck and shoulder.

And she lay there through it all, trying hard to feign sleep and not respond to his touch, while her mind raced for a plan.

She had underestimated both his stamina and his appetite, and Elsabeth now feared Cuncz would be able to go well into the night, and far too late for her to have time for a proper search. She had already attempted this ploy of pretending to be asleep several times as she tried to think of a way out, but he quickly learned just where to touch her to force her own body to betray her, which unfortunately made focusing on the task at hand something of a challenge. *Just my bloody luck to try this on someone who actually knows what he is doing in bed...*

His hand slid up her belly to caress the bottom of her breast once more, and she forced herself not to tense her body against the telltale stirring — impossible not to feel with the way his body pressed against the length of hers — announcing he was ready for her again. Elsabeth tried to force herself to ignore him as he fondled her, but his hand once more found the spot he was seeking. She choked back the low moan building in her throat, but her efforts to feign sleep would soon once more prove futile.

Then suddenly, his hand slipped back down to her belly, and he gave the ball of her shoulder a quick, nibbling kiss, and the bed behind her shifted as he left it.

Elsabeth strained her ears, and could just detect the soft padding of his bare feet as he circled around the bed in front of her, then the soft creaking of the floorboards as he made his way across the chamber. She risked cracking one eye open, and gave the scene a quick and cautious survey.

Through the hazy slit of her vision, she could see Cuncz silhouetted against the silver light of the moon streaming through the window as he threaded his arms through a robe. He wrapped the gown around himself and cinched it about his waist, then slid his feet into a pair of slippers, before quietly making his way to the far corner. If she rightly remembered what little of the layout of the room she saw in their mad scramble from the door to the bed (she blushed at the recollection they did not quite make it), it was the northwest corner. Rather than meeting at a right angle, as did the other corners of the chamber, the wall here turned to cut across the angle instead. A bookshelf stood against the wall, and he was regarding it thoughtfully. It was the only other furniture of note, besides the large bed she now occupied, and a quiet conversation circle of chairs around a low table in the room's northeast corner.

He cast a glance over his shoulder to where she lay, still unmoving with the blankets cast down around her waist, then turned his attention back to the bookshelf. He drew one of the volumes toward him and to her surprise a soft click, just audible over the whisper of her own breath, broke the stillness of the room. She could hear the faint creak of well-oiled hinges as the bookshelf pivoted into the room, revealing a black hole in the shadow of the wall. Cuncz gave her one last look, then silently slipped inside, and pulled it closed behind him.

She waited several tense moments, daring neither to move, nor even open her eyes fully, and strained her ears for any sign of activity in or near the solar. When no other sounds presented themselves, Elsabeth slipped from bed and quietly padded toward the bookshelf. Even knowing they were there, she could see no trace of the well-concealed hinges along its edge. She was amazed at the sheer number of volumes lined up on its shelves, most written in the Boehman tongue, but here and there she spied one in Navarrese, or her own native Coventrish, and still others she could not name. Their leather covers and bindings were used but well cared-for, except for one resting in the middle of the second shelf from the top, with a bright red leather spine, and gold letters in an unfamiliar language. Elsabeth reached out for it and stopped short. The bindings on this book certainly looked new, and stood out so well among the rest of the collection it easily drew the eye, and as she studied it she realized it perhaps did so too well. She took a cursory look at the other volumes, and smiled tightly as she looked at a tall manuscript to the left of the one she first reached for. On both its front and back cover she could just make out an arcing streak in the thin layer of dust the cleaning staff could not quite remove. Elsabeth took a firm grip and pulled the book toward her. It resisted a moment, then naturally pivoted on yet another masterfully disguised hinge before reaching a stop. She once again heard the same quiet click, before the bookshelf slowly swung away from the wall, and a dark, tightly spiraling stone stairwell yawned open in front of her. She chuckled softly.

"They always put them behind the bookcase," she said, as a chill gust of wind spiraled up out of the darkness and set her finer hairs on end. Elsabeth quickly withdrew to find her discarded chemise and shoes. She slipped into both, returned to the tunnel, and cautiously stepped onto the landing of the staircase inside. A handle on the back of the bookcase allowed it to be closed behind her and opened again from this side. A dim glow somewhere below her provided just enough illumination to make out the edge of the steps as they wound clockwise around a stone column supporting the ceiling of the passage. She tried the latch experimentally to be sure she could leave that way again, then carefully started down into the darkness.

The staircase descended sharply, but though it wound in a tight spiral, and the steps were narrow, they were even and well maintained, with no cracks or broken edges waiting to send her tumbling helplessly down to her death. However, it was still dark and steep, and Elsabeth needed one hand on the wall to keep her balance, while the other held up the skirt of her chemise to keep herself from tripping on it.

She descended past the level of the third floor of the central wing, then down through the second, and finally the first. There were no other exits she could readily see, and it appeared as if the passage connected the solar directly to whatever lay at its bottom. The staircase continued to spiral downward, and gradually the dim golden glow she first noted at the top of the passage resolved into the flicker of torches. The air here was thick with the acrid stench of burning pitch, and she heard them sputter and pop from somewhere just below her. As she reached the level of the cellars the brickwork walls gave way to bedrock, the temperature dropped noticeably, and the roughly-hewn stone walls of the lower level became cool and moist to the touch. Finally she reached the bottom and the staircase ended abruptly in a short tunnel roughly carved out of the surrounding stone. A sealed timber door, framed with iron, blocked passage any further. Torches placed in iron brackets on either side dimly illuminated this part of the tunnel.

Elsabeth crept to the door and placed her ear against it, and she clearly heard two separate voices. One belonged to Lord Cuncz, the other spoke gravely and with an air of authority.

"…do not see what was so important as to keep me waiting," the unidentified voice said. "I will not risk being missed."

"Calm yourself, father," Cuncz said. Elsabeth quirked an eyebrow. *Father?* "I was in the midst of entertaining a guest and it would have been rather unseemly for me to have her thrown from my solar in the middle of the night."

She heard the other make a sound that might have been a disgusted grunt. "What is more unseemly is your obsession with whatever passing harlot happens to catch your fancy."

Cuncz's voice turned angry. "Do mind your tongue, father. I will not have a guest in my home insulted. And I am sure you have not come from Friuli to comment upon my choice of company. What may I do for you?"

"There has been trouble at the Abbey," the other said, his voice quietly indignant over Cuncz's warning.

"I see. Are your brothers helping themselves to the sacramental wine, or perhaps taking a more...hands-on approach to the confessions of the female laity of late?"

The other made no attempt to disguise his indignation this time. "No such thing of the sort! Someone has broken into the

Abbey twice, and made off with the documents in my keeping. I recovered them once and the thieves were dealt with, but their co-conspirators must have gotten wind of the theft's failures and returned."

Ah, Father Garnerius. So Lord Cuncz is involved with whatever game the Abbot is playing.

"And you let them just walk right into the Abbey and take them again?" Cuncz's own voice turned concerned, but he kept the other's rising note of alarm out of his own speech.

"Of course not! I moved them to a compartment only I have access to."

Cuncz made a sound much like a short laugh. "Oh, of course. That only means it is perhaps the least secure place you could have put them. And since you are here now, clearly your security is more lacking than you realized. Who was it?"

"I do not know, but some agent of his Grace I suspect. We are still trying to determine how he even got in to the Abbey in the first place. After the first theft, I ordered the entire complex sealed while we dealt with the matter."

"And you wish to know if I had some agent of my own I could lend you to track him down?"

"Yes. And also to tell you that we will be delaying our plans until the documents are back in my possession."

"That is out of the question. You know the timetable we are on," Cuncz said. Elsabeth quirked an eyebrow and pressed her ear closer against the door.

"I do not need you to lecture me on expediency, boy," the Abbot snapped. "I have been working toward this for longer than you know, and I will not see it unravel over your impatience. This agent of the Bishop must be dealt with, and what he has stolen recovered, before word of it reaches his Grace. What have you done with the documents in your possession?"

Elsabeth's breath caught in her throat, and she listened intently.

"They are in the locked drawer of my desk in the study."

The Abbot grunted. "Ah yes, much more secure."

"Quite a bit, in fact. Had the first theft been mere thieves, anyone who would rob an Abbey would have gone right to that false reliquary you had them stashed in, thinking it was pure gold. And a skilled thief would know to look for your little hidey-hole, and would also know anything hidden away inside it was something of value, without being able to read it themselves. But just another stack of papers in a desk drawer? A casual thief would pay it no mind. An agent of the Bishop would need to be able to read them to know it was what he wanted. You would be surprised what people miss when it is in plain sight."

"All the same, I am done with having everything scattered about. I want it all moved to where it can be kept together and watched closely. I will send a man to collect them when I return to the Abbey."

"If you insist, Father.

"I do indeed, my son. I must take my leave. I must be on the road soon if I expect to reach Friuli before I am missed. I will let you return to your whore."

Elsabeth quickly scrambled away muttering quietly under her breath at the Abbot's insult. Now she knew where to look, and it was only a matter of arranging an opportunity to do so. She idly fingered the Wheel pendant around her neck as a plan took shape in her mind.

Chapter VII

She decided the passage must have another exit somewhere, as Cuncz's return came from an unexpected direction. Elsabeth waited for him in a small private dining hall on the upper level of the manor. It was located along the south face of the building, with tall windows looking out onto the bailey. A door in the northeast corner led to Cuncz's private study, and from there, to the solar on the left, or the bower on the right. A heavy timber trestle table, surrounded by chairs with padded leather seats and backs, dominated the center of the hall. A silver tray, with a bottle of more of the wine from dinner and two goblets, waited for them there. There were cupboards and shelves along the north and west walls for storing dishes and cutlery, and a fireplace occupied the eastern wall. Doors to the east and west led to halls allowing access to the rest of the central wing, and Cuncz returned through one of these to find her sitting on a rug laid out in front of the fireplace, while a small blaze crackled in the hearth.

She turned at the sound of his entrance, put on a welcoming smile, and rose quickly to her feet. She left her hair spilling freely down her back in a disheveled cascade of copper, and adjusted the neckline of her chemise to tease him with a glimpse of her breast. She left her shoes behind in the solar, and the polished wooden floorboards were cold and smooth beneath her bare feet as she padded over to him, threw herself into his arms, and kissed him deeply. If Cuncz's conversation with the Abbot left him distracted he did not show it, and he kissed her back fully and eagerly, his hands wandering down to her bottom and pulling her tightly against him. Elsabeth forced down the rising thrill of the kiss, and gently pushed herself away from him.

"And what are you doing out here, my dear?" Cuncz asked with playful suspicion.

Elsabeth ran a finger down his chest. "I awoke and you were gone. I came to find you and bring you back to bed, but a servant said you would return shortly." She flashed him a smoldering and inviting smile. "I hope you do not mind, but I asked him to fetch us a bottle of wine. Go and sit by the fire, my lord, I will bring it to you."

Cuncz smiled back at her and kissed the side of her neck, taking advantage of the moment of closeness for another grope of her backside, then made his way over to the fireplace. For a moment he left Elsabeth alone with the wine, and she needed little more time than that. She quickly filled both goblets, and then carefully turned the chain loop atop her Wheel pendant until she felt, more than heard, the soft metallic click as the hidden latch released, and the face of the pendant popped open. She pinched out a bit of the fine white powder within and sprinkled it into one of the goblets, then closed the pendant again with another barely-audible click. Elsabeth swirled the doctored wine, then returned to the fireplace.

She handed Cuncz his drink and lowered herself to the rug. Elsabeth adjusted her skirts as she folded her legs beneath her, and bared her lower legs for him. Cuncz took a swallow of his wine and shifted closer to her so he could run a hand along her calf. "I do apologize for leaving you so suddenly, my dear," he said, and took another long drink. His hand reached her knee, and slipped under her skirts to continue up her thigh. "A rather urgent matter needed my attention."

Elsabeth drank from her own goblet and allowed a giggle as his searching hand wandered to her hip, then began to inch over to the inside of her thigh. "I hope it was nothing serious." She swatted his shoulder playfully as his searching fingers edged even closer to the space between her legs.

He chuckled and took another drink from his goblet. "Not at all. And I swear, you now have my undivided attention."

Elsabeth smiled at him over the rim of her goblet. "Wonderful, I would hate for us to be interrupted further."

"Will you and your father be remaining in my humble town for long?"

She sighed heavily. "I fear not. My father prefers not to remain in any one market for long. He says it is poor business to sit in one place. I suspect he is already seeking a man to make arrangements with for the sale of his goods in Leyen."

"Ah, then perhaps I should have invited him to dinner as well. I prefer to keep a close eye on such arrangements myself. I find that there is much less incentive for such local contacts to cheat on the tariffs when I take a personal hand in the matter."

She made a pout. "But then I fear you and I would not have had as much time alone."

Cuncz reached out to stroke her leg again, and took another drink. He was slow in taking the goblet from his lips, and hesitated before responding. "Which I would have deeply regretted," he finally said after a moment, and when he did his words were ever so slightly slurred. "But if you will remain my guests another few days, perhaps I shall have time to speak with him before you depart."

"I believe we may still be here a few days more at least, perhaps a week."

"Excellent, all the better, since we shall have more time together. You will remain my personal guest here, of course."

Elsabeth giggled. "Of course."

Cuncz swayed a little, and mopped his brow with the back of his hand. "Wonderful! I will very much..." He trailed off suddenly, and his last words were so slurred together she could not make them out.

She allowed a look of concern to appear on her face. "My lord, are you all right?"

He slurred something more she could not understand, then slumped onto his elbow before collapsing onto his back. Cuncz's head lolled about, and his eyes glassed over as they gazed at the ceiling. Elsabeth casually drained the last of her wine and gave him a quick look, and satisfied herself that he was still breathing. "I am sorry about that, love, but had you only been concerned about your own pleasure and gone right to sleep when you popped off like I had counted on, we might have avoided this entirely," she said quietly into the stillness of the dining hall, and leaving Cuncz to lie unconscious next to the fire, headed for the study.

The private study was a chamber of modest size and not particularly opulent in its furnishings. A single wooden desk dominated the center of the room. In one corner sat a couch and two chairs around a table, a map of Leyen's surroundings hung on a board on the wall to her left as she entered, and shelves laden with books, scrolls, and other odds and ends occupied the wall immediately to her right. A row of curtained windows looked out to the north across the bailey, and she could see the fading light of the moon glistening on the waters of the river in the darkness outside.

Paintings, whose details she could not make out in the faint moonlight, hung on the east and west walls.

Elsabeth hurried over to the desk and quickly checked the drawers until she found the locked one Cuncz had mentioned to the Abbot. She slipped a hand into a pocket hidden within her chemise, withdrew the leather pouch for her lock picks, and quickly went to work. It took only a few moments for the lock to click, and she pulled the drawer open and began to search through the stacks of papers within. Most were innocuous documents of little interest: correspondence with merchants and other nobles, trade ledgers, inventories, records of wages for the manor's staff, minutes from meetings of the town's council, and other miscellanea. Finally, buried at the very bottom of the drawer in a leather case, she found what she was looking for, a nondescript sheaf of papers bearing the seal of Father Garnerius. Elsabeth stuffed them down the front of her chemise, returned the empty leather case and other papers to where she found them, and slid the drawer closed. The lock clicked on its own, and she gathered up her picks, retrieved her shoes from the solar, and hurried toward the door leading back into the private dining hall.

As she emerged from the study, she found the Chamberlain leaning over the prostrate form of Lord Cuncz, with three guards behind him, all turning to look in her direction as she stepped into the room.

"Oh bollocks," she said.

"Seize her!" Conrat said, and the three guards charged her, drawing swords as they came.

Elsabeth retreated quickly into the study, seized its heavy timber door in both hands, and swung it closed into the face of the first guard to reach her. It struck him hard and he stumbled backwards under the force of the blow, entangling himself with his comrades and sending the entire group crashing to the floor snarling curses in her direction. She wasted no time in taking advantage of the distraction, and coiling her legs beneath her, sprung back into the dining hall and dove over the guards as they fought to free themselves from each other's limbs. She struck on her shoulder and rolled back to her feet in time to meet a panicked dagger-stroke from the astonished Chamberlain. She lunged to her left and guided his attack past her right shoulder with her forearm, and used his own momentum coming forward to throw him over her leg and into the recovering guards.

Elsabeth turned and ran for the fireplace, sprung over Cuncz, and snatched a poker from a rack of tools next it as she fled past. She rushed for the east door and hurriedly pulled it shut behind her as she fled into the hall, slid the poker through the handle, and wedged both ends as best she could into the frame, before hurrying on her way again. She found herself in a short hall that ended in a dead end on her left. To her right the hall ended at a flight of stairs leading down to the galleries overlooking the great hall. Across from her were narrow windows draped with velvet curtains, looking out eastward a good two stories above the east wing. A short distance away she could make out the shadow of the tower at that end of the manor, black against the indigo of the dying night sky.

The door behind her shook as someone yanked on its handle. She heard the squeak of the poker digging into the wooden frame as it began to give way under the effort of the guards trying to force it open, each tug on the handle from inside opening the crack between the edge of the door and the jamb just a little wider. Elsabeth let out a decisive breath and hurried to the window closest to the center of the roof below her, finding them locked with only a simple latch. She flipped it and threw the window open. A warm breeze from the bailey greeted her as she peered out and looked down. The roof of the wing below was rather steeply peaked. Elsabeth turned suddenly at another squeal behind her, and found the door had opened wide enough that one of the guards was able to slip his hand through to try removing the poker from where it was wedged. "Bugger," she said, and quickly decided on her exit.

The windows were narrow and it took a little wiggling to clear her hips, but she was soon crouched in the windowsill with the curtain in hand. She made the sign of the Wheel, held her breath and dropped off. For a moment she fell freely, then she reached the end of her slack and kicked her legs to throw her weight forward, aiming to swing near enough to the center of the roof so she could grab hold of the ridge and stop herself from sliding down into empty space. The curtain began to tear free under her weight, and Elsabeth's momentum carried her right into the wall of the central wing. She grunted from the impact and lost her hold of the curtain, falling awkwardly the rest of the way to the roof below.

One foot touched down first and to her dismay she went down on her rear, the ridge just out of reach as she went skidding backwards and downwards. She managed to roll herself onto her belly and grabbed at the shingles with one hand to swing around until she was sliding feet-first. She bit back tears of pain as she dug her fingertips into the roof in hopes of gaining purchase. Instead, she slid all the way off the end of the roof, and it was only when her hands caught the gutter that she managed to stop her slide.

The sudden stop jolted her shoulders and she cried out as her fingers found a grip on the edge of the channel. For a moment she hung there, before looking both ways along the roof. The eavesdrip was too far out from the wall, and the windows too far down, for her to safely climb inside from here, and the roof itself was too steep for her to climb back up again. She was too far from the east tower to make her way in that direction, particularly in the time she had before Conrat could rouse the guard, and there was nowhere toward the main wing where she could reach another window, or find a handhold, to climb down. Elsabeth looked down, and saw the ground immediately beneath her, two stories down, was a lawn of grass.

"Bugger it," she said, and released her grip, throwing her weight around to face away from the wall.

The fall ended with alarming suddenness. As Elsabeth's feet struck the ground she allowed her legs to collapse under her and threw herself forward into a roll. She tumbled across the ground, arms shielding her head and neck, and stopped herself with a break fall. She checked herself for injury, but a quick survey revealed nothing more serious than fingertips scraped and bloodied from trying to stop her slide down the roof, and a few bruises from the fall. Elsabeth double-checked the documents hidden away in her chemise and looked about quickly for a means of escape before the alarm was raised.

Only one gate led out of the inner bailey, and this was under guard, to say nothing of the men patrolling beyond. Elsabeth kept to the wall of the manor and used its shadow to hide as best she could from the guards on the battlements, as she quickly edged her way toward the east tower. She rounded it quickly to the back side of the building, and spied a well in the narrow court between the back of the manor and the inner wall, normally accessed by a door leading from the kitchens behind the great hall. No one stood watch at the door, though a lantern on either side of the entrance lit the surrounding area. She hurried as quickly as caution allowed across the court and gave the well a quick looking over.

It was a simple brick shaft with a winch used to raise the heavy wooden bucket, now resting on the rim of the well, and draw water from below. She could not see how deeply it descended, but with the river near at hand, Elsabeth guessed there might be some stream branch that cut under the hill, though whether its entrance and exit was above the surface of the water she would not be able to tell until she found it. From around the front of the manor she heard the sound of voices shouting orders; one, at least, was Conrat, and with no other options, she let the barrel drop into the shaft, sprinted to the door to grab one of the lanterns, and rushed back to the well. Elsabeth seated herself on the edge, grabbed hold of the rope, and swung herself into the hole. The drop of the bucket suddenly accelerated under her weight, and the dim circle of the sky above vanished as she plummeted into the darkness.

Elsabeth did not bother to keep the time of her fall, and only the splash of the bucket hitting the water told her when it reached the bottom. She descended a moment more herself, when suddenly the rope attached to the winch above played out and she snapped to an abrupt stop that tore her hand from the rope, and with a cry of alarm she fell backwards into the water below. It was quite deep and icy cold, and Elsabeth shot back to the surface with a gasp. Unfortunately, she lost her lantern when she hit the water, and as she righted herself and found the rope again she was left in darkness.

Elsabeth allowed herself a moment for her eyes to adjust to the dark and to get her bearings. The faint circle of moonlight shining into the well revealed she had descended into a cistern lined with brick, and the water flowed past her, fed by some channel dug off the river. She could just make out a raised walkway running the circumference of the cistern, but the rest was lost in total blackness. Elsabeth swam in that direction and hauled herself out of the water. She shivered in the darkness, turning first one way and then another, listening intently for any sign of pursuit. *Well, this whole adventure will have been pointless if those papers are ruined. No time to do anything about that now, though.*

Elsabeth chose to follow the flow of water, carefully feeling her way along the wall. The walkway was dry and the brickwork was masterfully done. She guessed the river seldom reached higher than its current level, and even in flood would normally be below the level of the walkway. Her spirits lifted: Surely this channel and the cistern saw regular maintenance, and anyone who came down here would have another means of entering than the one she chose.

The passage ran straight and level for some distance, until it ended at a blank wall of bedrock where she suspected the canal exited to rejoin the river by means of a grated opening somewhere deep below the surface. She felt around the surrounding walls seeking an exit, and her searching hands found a heavy timber and iron-bound door near at hand. She cautiously tugged on the handle and found it locked, but she needed only a moment with her picks to have it open. Not a shred of light from beyond escaped the crack beneath the door or through its keyhole. Elsabeth fumbled in the dark for the door handle and pulled experimentally. It gave easily and noiselessly, and she slipped into the darkened chamber beyond and shut the door behind her, where it clicked locked again.

A thin silver light shone in through a narrow window somewhere high overhead. It mingled with the golden light of torches casting flickering shadows on the walls, and she realized she must be at the bottom of one of the towers ringing the outer bailey. Stacked crates and boxes, barrels, tools, and other supplies stored here, along with a dozen or so feet of rope coiled on a box, filled the space beneath the spiraling staircase leading up into the tower. Elsabeth hung the rope over her shoulder, then started as quickly and quietly as she could up the staircase. After a few stories, she cautiously approached a landing at ground level, where a heavy iron-bound door allowed access to the tower from the bailey. When she saw it was deserted, she hurried past and continued up. She passed several arrow loops, their embrasures too narrow for her to slip through, until she finally reached a small open window about halfway up the tower. The only place she found to secure her rope was an iron bracket bearing one of the torches filling the tower with muted light and a good deal of acrid smoke. Elsabeth made her line fast about the bracket, then with a great deal of effort squeezed through the window. It was a very close fit, and she very nearly caught her hips in the window frame before she finally managed to wriggle through. She was soon rappelling down the tower and muttering to herself about making yet another long descent.

Fortunately, this time her feet reached the ground before the end of her lifeline, and she took off from the cover of the wall, her ears alert for shouts of alarm and warning. She heard the commotion raised by the search of the grounds growing as the guards shifted their attention to the outer bailey, but for the moment she found herself clear, where the wall of the town intersected with the outer wall of the manor. The rise on which she now stood descended a steep bluff toward the river below, and Elsabeth quickly slipped out of sight of the walls and onto the slope. She picked a careful path down to the edge of the water, and angled off to meet Hieronymus.

Chapter VIII

"You are late, girl," he said, when she finally arrived at their meeting place near the west bridge. Fortunately, Hieronymus had the good sense to choose a place somewhat out of sight of the guards patrolling the town walls and those stationed at the gate itself. Her clothes were wet, and to her consternation she was suddenly aware the white linen of her chemise was no longer entirely opaque. As the excitement of her flight faded, her bumps and bruises started to ache, but the night was warm and her hurts were not serious. Still, she limped slightly and was glad for an opportunity to sit and rest for a moment.

"Hello to you, too," she said once she caught her breath, then winced and got back to her feet. "Come on, we better be long gone from here before first light."

"Run into some trouble, then?"

"You of all people should know I am always in trouble. But the more miles we put between us and Leyen, the better." She levered herself to her feet. "We have a little time at least before the search gets really persistent, I think. Lord Cuncz should not wake from his little nap until well into tomorrow."

She limped over to where Hieronymus had left her belongings, grabbed her sword, slung its baldric over her shoulder, gathered up her pack, and started off. "Well, I guess you really are that good, eh?" he said as he watched her.

Elsabeth glanced over her shoulder and flashed him a mischievous smile. "Oh I am. But he was even better."

Hieronymus's step faltered at that. "Well, that would explain your limping then."

"No, the limp is from falling off the roof. Or down the well. Or maybe I strained something climbing out of that tower window. I really have had a rather long night and would like at least a few hours sleep at some point. So let us just get as far as we can, and find a good place to set camp. If luck is with us, the papers I found will still be legible if all the ink has not run off them first."

They turned north into the plains once the walls of Leyen were out of sight behind them, and marched for two or three hours in that direction. A rosy blush appeared on the horizon to the east as night slowly loosened its grip on the world and gave way to dawn. The stars winked out and faded, and the sky brightened. The flat land northwest of the town left them with no cover, and they avoided the huts of the serfs who worked Cuncz's fields, so they were obliged to stop for the night and set camp out in the open. They made no fire, and Elsabeth merely laid out her bedroll, threw herself down, and fell right to sleep.

She awoke again only a few hours later. Hieronymus still snored in his bedroll opposite her, giving Elsabeth time to slip a short ways away and change into her traveling clothes. She returned to their camp, adjusting the hang of her sword at her hip and the rondel at her back, to find the friar seated and watching her with a smirk. "Letch," she said as she returned to her bedroll, and threw herself down.

"I was just admiring what the Lord of All saw fit to grace the world with when you slipped from the womb. There is no harm at all in taking just a peak," he said. "I certainly hope last night was worth all the trouble."

She flashed him a wicked smile. "Oh, it was. We went for hours and hours. In fact the first time we did not even make it to the bed and he took me right there on the floor."

Hieronymus glared at her. "Now that is just being cruel, Tetty."

Elsabeth did not let him off so easily. "It really was amazing, perhaps the best I ever had. I might still be there now if we did not have a job to do."

"I am sure with your impressive history you will find someone to make you forget about him soon enough," he said. "The body is a sacred temple crafted by the Lord himself. You have turned yours into the village fair."

"And you have dedicated yours to waving your staff about in every nunnery from Soest to Navarre," she said. Elsabeth opened the papers, actually, many sheets of vellum, taken from Cuncz's desk as she spoke, unfolded them, and spread them out so she could examine them. Fortunately, the damage caused by her unexpected fall into the well was not serious, and the text was still clearly legible, written in a bold and elegant hand with black ink only slightly faded from age. She skimmed over the first, then the second, with an ever-increasing arch of her eyebrow as she studied the seven pages of the document.

"These are the papers of adoption and legitimation of Cuncz drawn up at Rupertus's orders. Father Garnerius was a signatory and witness to all of them," she said.

Hieronymus frowned. "Curious, I was not given the understanding the Abbot had such close contact with Lord Rupertus."

"Considering our employer asked us to investigate the connection in the first place, it seems that might have been the idea. It slipped my mind in all the excitement, but Garnerius was here in Leyen last night. Cuncz left me alone in bed in the middle of the night to meet with him in secret. If I need to make the connection for you, this would be that mysterious visitor those fellows at the inn mentioned being received at the castle late at night."

The friar harrumphed and fixed her with a particularly indignant look. "My mental faculties are quite up to the task of coming to such a conclusion without your assistance, you irreverent harpy."

She tapped the top sheet against the others thoughtfully. "Oh good, and here I thought you would only slow me down. Well, Cuncz thought I was still asleep and did not realize I followed him to his meeting. Father Garnerius certainly seemed insistent that these documents be removed to somewhere more secure before something happened to them." Elsabeth smirked at Hieronymus. "Pity Lord Cuncz was a bit preoccupied last night."

"Yes," he said. "Quite the pity. If you are finished with your fond reminiscences over your unseemly nocturnal escapades, we are rather exposed out here. If you have some idea of where to go next, I would rather love to hear it."

"A moment," she said, and looked over the documents once more. "There is a second witness on all of these documents. A Father Ehrhart. Do you know him?"

He twisted his mouth in a scowl. "Ah, yes, because all of the clergy clearly took their vows together, so we must all know one another personally. No I do not know him, though I can say at least

I do know of him. As I recall, Ehrhart is prior of Alsfeld Monastery. That is about a two day walk east of Leyen, on the north bank of the river."

Elsabeth folded the documents again and stuffed them in a pouch on her pack. "Well, that sounds as good a place as any to turn next."

"You are forgetting that means we must walk right past Leyen. And while it is a two-day march on foot, even the Right Reverend Garnerius's fat arse can beat us there by horse with plenty of time to hold communion for all the brothers while he waited."

She shook her head. "Garnerius would be well on his way back to Friuli Abbey by now. He made it plain to Cuncz he needed to return before he would be missed this morning. I think Cuncz's chamberlain would be in charge of any pursuit until he finishes sleeping off the drug I gave him, and may delay a serious one until he does. I suspect they would also send a messenger to the Abbey as well, which may mean another delay, especially if the Chamberlain does not know about these..." she patted her pouch "...and would not be expecting us to double back and head that way."

Elsabeth got back to her feet and packed up her bedroll. "That gives us a small head start, at least. I think we should hurry and take advantage of it while we have the time."

Hieronymus grumbled his dissent as they hurriedly packed up their camp, but reluctantly accepted her decision. Soon they were off again, turning east but keeping away from the river, until well after they passed Leyen again to their right. They saw no one as they cut across the fields, and as they finally rejoined the river they stepped out onto a road. It was little more than a flattened, hard, and badly-rutted dirt track with ill-defined grassy edges that followed the course of the broad waterway as it wound out of the east on its journey past Leyen. In places the water cut back and forth across the road, which either forded it when shallow, or spanned the deeper parts on bridges constructed of brick, and were the only stretches that were well maintained. At other times, the road veered off to skirt bogs and marshes where the river turned in wide, slow bends, before returning to follow its true course again. Somewhere east of Leyen the cleared fields gave way to woodland, and the road turned away from the river to climb onto higher and dryer ground. The hiss of wind through the trees gathering around the road, and the singing of birds, was a lively change of pace from the still land outside the forest. However, it made listening for pursuit on the road a challenge, and the stands of trees and surrounding undergrowth greatly diminished their ability to spot trouble approaching.

Nonetheless, the two days of travel passed uneventfully, and by the end of the second day they reached a fork in the road. Hieronymus led her on the southern branch, which emerged from the woodland and wound its way unerringly back toward the river through pasture and farmland, as it climbed a rise to a bluff overlooking the water that lay fifty or so feet below. Perched atop this bluff, behind a thick and rather low wall of stone, was Alsfeld Monastery.

Beyond the wall was an outer court with guest houses, servants' quarters, and a few other storage buildings and workshops, along with ponds, gardens, and a dairy. Separated from this by a hedge was the inner court and its laundries, infirmaries, bakehouses, a brewery, granaries, and stables. The claustral dominated the heart of the inner court. The church rose prominently at the north end, with ranges on the east, west and southern faces to enclose the cloister. The main gatehouse was a sturdy two-level structure, but the outer wall was merely for purposes of privacy, and would never stand against even a half-hearted assault.

Hieronymus leaned on his staff, with a pendant of the Wheel displayed prominently around his neck, as they approached the gate and awaited the guard to clear them for entry. The guard was a rather short and scrawny older man with a weathered face, and dressed in a faded linen gambeson under a well-worn brigandine. He wore a dagger at his back, and a crude-looking axe with a short haft was at his belt. He regarded Hieronymus with bored indifference. His eyes then wandered Elsabeth's body for a moment longer than proper, and he scowled at the sword at her hip.

"By command of Father Ehrhart, your arms must be surrendered at the gate before I can admit you," he said in a very official and automatic tone. Hieronymus gave up his sword and buckler, and handed both over to another guard who appeared from a staircase leading up to the second level overhead. Elsabeth took a quick look up, and saw no sign of murder-holes or a portcullis; only the timber gate denied entrance to or from the monastery. She reluctantly handed her sword over to the second guard.

"Do be careful with that," she said, a note of warning in her voice. "If I do not find it again when I return, the good prior will need to find two new guards." Elsabeth started to follow Hieronymus through, but the gate guard stopped her.

"Half a moment," he said. Irritation over her threat was evident in his voice, and he stepped into her path. She stood a good head taller than him, and even with her lithe build, Elsabeth suspected she still outweighed him. The guard casually strolled up to her, and soon had his hands on her, running them the length of her body and groping her with the excuse of seeking hidden weapons. When his searching fingers went to her backside, Elsabeth tired of the game and in one smooth motion twisted his arm around, flung him up against the gate, and pinned him there by the sleeve of his gambeson with her rondel.

"I trust you are satisfied?" she said with a glare.

The guard removed her dagger from the gate and freed himself, and with a huff strode over and handed it to his companion before angrily waving her through. Elsabeth nodded curtly and joined Hieronymus inside, casting a glance over her shoulder to watch their weapons taken up to the second floor of the gatehouse. "Charming as always," Hieronymus muttered as he led her along the path through the outer court.

Elsabeth scowled down at him. "Oh do not give me that, you saw how he had his hands on me."

"I thought you enjoyed being pawed by every strange man you came across."

"Only by invitation."

"You did threaten him."

"I merely wished to make it clear how unhappy I will be if my sword is not where I left it when we come back."

"Yes, two guards are completely worth a sword."

She spit him with a warning glare. "That one is to me, and you know better than to say anything more about it."

Hieronymus shrugged, and they continued the rest of the way in silence. There were a few lay people in the outer court, most of them servants running errands for the complex up ahead or tending to the grounds, gardens, and workshops. All of them ignored the pair as they made their way along a path paved with white cobblestones, and bordered with beds of yellow and white flowers. Elsabeth saw no sign of guards other than those at the gate, and the outer court was silent.

The inner court was another matter entirely. Everywhere she looked, Elsabeth saw children, and a dull ache filled her heart at the sight. All were boys, ranging in age from a few years old to nearly early manhood. The eldest helped watch over the youngest under the close eye of the brothers of the monastery, though the boys all appeared to be laity and dressed in simple, and at times worn and well-used clothing. Some sat in circles around the brothers as they lectured on diverse subjects; in one corner of the court she even caught a glimpse of a brother giving lessons on the sword and buckler, while another wielded a staff in what looked to be a variation on the teachings of Russdorffer (at which Elsabeth rolled her eyes). Others were engaged in a variety of exercise, particularly games of chase and other sports. Hieronymus chuckled warmly in greeting whenever such games spilled over onto the path, and the children greeted him with solemn nods and "beg your pardons" before rushing off to begin their games all over again. Elsabeth quickly became a subject of intense scrutiny and spectacle, and many stopped what they were doing to stare as she passed. She forced aside the deep pang of sorrow and smiled in return.

Elsabeth followed Hieronymus as he approached the church. It was a modest structure two stories in height. The eastern end was a round structure with a dome roof, and a long axis stretching toward the façade at the west end. The east range met the church at the center of this rounded structure, with a small side door exiting into the courtyard to the north directly opposite. The façade extended a few dozen feet beyond the wall of the west range with yet another small side door to the inner court opposing it. At each corner of the façade stood a tower four stories in height, framing a porch mounted by a short flight of three steps. Most of the building was in the ubiquitous red brick, but the façade was made of white stone, with its three processional doors mounted in marble archways, all carved and decorated with sculpture.

Hieronymus climbed the stairs onto the porch and made his way to the middle door, which stood open to let in light and the summer breeze. They passed through, and entered a vestibule with a floor of colored tiles and plastered walls. Doors at either hand led to the corner towers, and marble fonts stood at either side of the doors leading into the nave. Elsabeth and Hieronymus stopped, dipped their fore and middle fingers into the water, and made the sign of the Wheel before proceeding.

"I am rather surprised you did not burst into flames just now," Hieronymus muttered as they entered the nave. It ran in a long central aisle down the center of the church, with a floor of imported stone, a vaulted ceiling supported by a frame of carved and painted timbers, and an arcade separated the central aisle from a lower aisle on either side. A transept bisected the large circular chamber at the far end, with doors leading to the east range and the inner court opposite, and just beyond this stood the rood separating the nave and chancel. Even further beyond this, screened off and out of sight by the rood, lay the sanctuary where the altar and Tabernacle were kept. Carved timber columns supported the arcade separating the aisles of the nave, and a carpet ran the length of the floor, disappearing beneath the rood. Sunlight filtered in through a skylight in the dome over the crossing, and through the large windows of stained glass at the apse, formed as the walls of the main circular chamber came together beyond the transept.

She did not bother turning her eyes on him after his remark, and instead swept her gaze across the church as they followed the carpet down the nave. A young novice, in a habit of brown wool, with plain boyish features and a mop of sandy hair, tending to the church saw them, and started toward them. "This is hardly the place to hound me about my sins, considering you have a list long enough to astound the Lord of All himself," she muttered back. Even with her lowered voice her words were amplified much more than Elsabeth cared for, but if the novice heard her he did not show it as he reached them and bowed in greeting, though he eyed Elsabeth somewhat uncertainly.

No Good Deed...

"Welcome to Alsfeld, and may the blessings of the Lord be upon you, is there anything I may do to assist you, Brother?" he said pleasantly to Hieronymus, then almost as an afterthought turned to Elsabeth and inclined his head. "Milady?"

Hieronymus stretched to his full height, and took on a very proper and regal air. "Yes, there is. I have a need to speak with Father Ehrhart, do run along and fetch him for me."

The novice stumbled a moment at Hieronymus's rather brusque request, and he hesitated to find his voice. "I am sorry, Brother, but Father Ehrhart is in private prayer and asked not to be disturbed."

The friar spit the younger man with a glare, and a hint of authoritative anger slipped into his voice. "Now look here my son, I have not traveled all this way from my province to be thrown out on my backside by a novice who only just received his habit."

Elsabeth struggled to keep the smirk from her lips as the youth flinched back in surprise, and he broke down into a fit of stuttering. "I shall have a meal and a place to rest from your journey prepared for yourself and your companion while you wait, but Father Ehrhart is simply unable to see you—"

Hieronymus cut him off. "Oh enough of this," he said, and started off down the nave. "I will go and see him myself. The dormitories are in the west range, as I recall? And I shall have a word with the good Father about the quality of his brothers for keeping important business from him."

The novice followed as Hieronymus made his way along the aisle toward the transept, babbling and practically tripping over his habit in an effort to cut the friar off. "Wait. Wait! Please, just a moment! I will see if he has a moment he can spare, but I must insist you wait here!"

He stopped and regarded the novice, somehow managing to look down his nose at the younger man, though the latter nearly towered well over him. "Very well, but I have little time to waste, this matter is of the utmost urgency, and needs his attention immediately."

"Yes, Brother, I will go at once. Lord be with you," he said, bowing fervently and hurrying from the church. Elsabeth watched him go, then shook her head and rolled her eyes.

"You do know they are building a special hall in the Underworld for you," she said.

Hieronymus merely shrugged. "Just remember coming here was your idea, Tetty. And besides, we do have little time. Your dearest love can still catch us here before we can leave, or might be here already, and that rascal could have been told to keep us busy."

"Well, if he is, I promise we will wait until we are out of the church to tear each other's clothes off. God forbid we desecrate it with our lust."

"At least now you are thinking sensibly."

"One of us has to. Just remember I blame you for all of this."

After several minutes the novice returned, trailing behind an older figure, dressed in a similar habit of brown wool, but tied at his waist with a belt of braided gold and red cords. He was a tall man with a short, neatly-trimmed silver beard, who wore his silver hair cropped short. Father Ehrhart made his way along the transept and then turned down the nave with a purposeful stride. The novice following in his wake struggled to keep pace. He slowed as he approached, and stuffed his hands into the opposite sleeves of his habit as he drew nearer. Hieronymus inclined his head respectfully in greeting, and Elsabeth followed in suit.

"Well?" Ehrhart said, his voice a blend of curiosity over the urgency of the summons, and mild annoyance over the disruption of his church and claustral.

"Greetings, Father Ehrhart, and thank you for seeing us on such sudden notice," Hieronymus said. "I am Hieronymus, a brother of the Order of St. Olivus and I am here on a matter of some urgency."

"Yes, so Brother Auberlin has said. You certainly gave him quite a fright, Brother Hieronymus. Perhaps this has become common among the Olivians, but our novices here are not accustomed to such...fire. Nor of having to interrupt the private prayers of their superiors." The last he added with a pointed glare, which Hieronymus ignored.

"I beg your pardon, Father, but as I said, the matter is something of an urgent one. May we speak in private?"

Ehrhart heaved an impatient sigh, then waved toward a door in the middle of the nave on the south wall. "Brother Auberlin, see to it that we are not disturbed. I trust that this time you will not have difficulties obeying my instructions?"

Auberlin swallowed visibly and his face paled. "Yes, Father. I mean, no, Father. I mean..."

"Yes, yes, I know what you mean." He rolled his eyes and motioned for Hieronymus to follow, but as his eyes fell on Elsabeth, he frowned at her and hesitated. "It is not our practice to permit women to set foot in the cloister."

She opened her mouth to protest, but Hieronymus spoke first. "My companion, Elsabeth Soesten," he said in introduction. Elsabeth inclined her head in greeting. "She is assisting me with the matter on which I have come, and will be quite necessary in our discussion. I will take full responsibility for her if you require it of me."

Ehrhart regarded the pair for a moment, then heaved another sigh and nodded. "Very well. Come."

Ehrhart led them through the door, and they stepped into the cloister itself. An arcaded walkway encircled the garth, a lawn of green grass with a pool at its center, and separated it from the walls of the church and ranges enclosing it. The sun hung high overhead in a clear blue sky, dotted here and there with the occasional cloud. Elsabeth could hear the laughter of the children playing in the inner court beyond the claustral, and forced aside the hollow feeling that gnawed her gut at the sound. There was no one else about, and they followed Ehrhart as he made his way to the pool, where he waited for them to speak.

"I have noticed, Father, quite a large number of children seem to reside here at Alsfeld," Hieronymus began. "Are they here to devote themselves to the King of All?"

"No," Ehrhart said, "Not all. Some will eventually choose this path, as poor Brother Auberlin did. The others we keep here because they have no one else to care for them."

"Alsfeld is an orphanage then?" Elsabeth said.

Ehrhart looked sharply at her, and she keenly felt just how unwelcome her presence within the cloister was. "That is one of the services we offer here, yes, aside from our own studies and devotion to the Lord. And if you have intruded on my private prayers only to prattle on about the unfortunates in our care, then I must kindly ask you to leave."

Elsabeth set her pack down on the grass and removed the documents. "We are here at the request of an agent of his Grace the Prince-Bishop," Hieronymus said. "The trail has led us to your gates, and we wished to ask about something rather curious." Elsabeth handed the stack of vellum over to the prior who studied them with a frown.

"Where did you get these?"

"Under the circumstances, it would be better if you did not know," Elsabeth said. "But you do recognize them?"

"I do. These are the documents of adoption and legitimation drawn up by Lord Rupertus of Leyen when he adopted a son here."

Elsabeth frowned. "Lord Cuncz was adopted from here?"

Ehrhart glanced up from one of the pages at her. "That is what I said, is it not? I witnessed the adoption myself, accounting for my signature. Father Garnerius of Friuli Abbey was present as well."

Hieronymus leaned on his staff and watched the prior carefully. "Quite a ways for a man of Father Garnerius' stature to come to witness an adoption, is it not?"

The other grunted as he shuffled through the documents page by page, before returning them to Elsabeth. She in turn slipped them back into her pack and slung it over her shoulder once again. "Father Garnerius has had a personal interest in Lord Cuncz from the start. It was he who delivered him as a babe to Alsfeld, and personally arranged for his care and education. He visited from time to time to check in on his health and the progress of his education. And then to arrange his adoption and legitimation by Lord Rupertus."

Elsabeth raised an eyebrow. "That does not strike you as unusual?"

Ehrhart sighed. "Less so than you might think. I have seen many boys come through here of uncertain parentage who, I suspect, have family nearer at hand than they themselves know. There are simply some among the clergy who do not take their vows as seriously as they ought, while the bishops turn a blind eye, or indulge in it themselves."

She suppressed a laugh in Hieronymus's direction. He glared at her in silent warning, as if sensing the humor she found in that remark, but Ehrhart showed no sign of noticing either of their reactions. "What can you tell us about Cuncz's parents?" she said instead.

"Almost nothing aside that his mother was an unwed laywoman, I am afraid. Father Garnerius brought him here personally, and of his mother I was given no name."

"Do you know where she could be found?"

"The churchyard of Friuli Abbey," he said. "She died in childbirth, and if she were buried in a common grave then I suspect there is no purpose in searching further for her."

"When was Cuncz brought to the Abbey?"

Ehrhart considered for a moment. "It would have been the spring of 1414, as I recall."

Elsabeth folded her arms across her chest and glanced at Hieronymus. "Well, I do think it is rather odd Father Garnerius would take such a personal interest in Lord Cuncz, would you agree?"

Hieronymus nodded his agreement. "Most unusual, Tetty. One might almost say suspiciously so."

Ehrhart looked between the two of them and a frown of disapproval creased his features. "What is the meaning of this? You say you are here in the name of his Grace the Bishop, yet all you do is pry into the private affairs of Lord Cuncz. And do I miss my guess in suggesting those documents you brought were stolen?"

"What his Grace knows of all this is beyond me to say," Elsabeth said. "Only that we are acting under the instruction of an agent in his employ. Now perhaps Father Garnerius is merely a dirty old monk who could not keep his crosier under his habit—"

"Elsabeth!" Hieronymus said, a look of genuine mortification on his face.

"—but I do know for certain I have woken to an assassin standing over my bed, and I have fallen down a privy shaft, off a roof, down a well, and jumped out of a tower, and I am bloody well wanting to know what all of this is about. So forgive me for my sins, Father, but I think a little bit of thievery at this point might be a slight bit justifiable."

The prior opened his mouth as if to issue a retort, when a sudden commotion from behind spun her around and sent her reaching for the sword that was not at her hip. Brother Auberlin ran as swiftly as his long habit allowed him, crying, "Father Ehrhart! Father Ehrhart!" with an alarmed expression on his face. He stopped and doubled over to catch his breath. "Father Ehrhart!" he said again.

Ehrhart sighed patiently. "Yes, Brother Auberlin? I thought I asked we not be disturbed?"

"Yes, Father." Auberlin's face colored abruptly at the rebuke, "But Father Garnerius is here with Lord Cuncz, and they demand to speak with you."

Hieronymus's face drained of color, and Elsabeth muttered a subdued "Bollocks," after which she quickly made the sign of the Wheel.

"And what is the purpose of their visit?" Ehrhart said, his voice was calm, but Elsabeth saw the corners of his eyes tighten.

"Them, Father." Auberlin needlessly raised a hand to indicate her and Hieronymus. "He said two thieves might be headed this direction to hide in the monastery. Thieves, Father!" Auberlin leveled a suspicious glare on them which Elsabeth found almost comically misplaced on his youthful features.

"And what did you tell them?"

"That you were attending to a private meeting, and that you requested not to be disturbed, but it is Father Garnerius and the Baron, Father. They insisted. And rather officially, at that."

"Lord Cuncz bears no authority within these walls and he well knows it." Ehrhart sighed. "Father Garnerius, however, is another matter. Tell them I will join them shortly. Take them to my office in the south tower and see that they are comfortable."

Auberlin shifted uncomfortably at the thought of going back in to address the Abbot, but nodded. "Yes, Father."

"And say nothing of our guests, understood?"

"Yes, Father!"

"Good, now go."

Auberlin bowed stiffly at the waist, and hurried back to the church. Elsabeth distantly hoped that Garnerius and Cuncz did not choose to follow him, or heard the racket made by the young novice in his panic. Ehrhart turned to them and studied them sternly for a moment. "Now, what to actually do with you two," he said.

Hieronymus drew himself up to his full height and gazed back at the prior. "We have reason to believe that Father Garnerius is up to something against the wishes of his Grace, though what that may be, we cannot say. Part of the proof is already in the hands of our contact. It may be nothing, but I trust this man speaks the truth as to his association, and we have seen firsthand that there is some sinister game the Abbot is playing. If the Right Reverend has committed a crime, his Grace will wish to see all of the evidence we have found."

"It may take some time to sort out all that you are telling me, with what I am sure will be a wildly different tale Father Garnerius will tell. The south range is often empty this time of day, and its door is always open to guests, to come and go as they please. You might enjoy the privacy there while I meet with Lord Cuncz and Garnerius."

Hieronymus bowed low. "Blessings of the Lord be upon you, Father, for your time. Come, Tetty, let us see what refreshment we may find there." He started off toward the south range. Elsabeth bowed to Ehrhart, and excused herself politely before following after him.

Chapter IX

"Well, you are just performing one sacrilege after another today," she said, as she stepped out of the range and into the inner court, the woolen habit of a monk slipped on over the rest of her clothes, and her long copper tresses tucked away inside a cowl.

"Oh pipe down, Tetty," Hieronymus said from within his own hood. "You have taken a vow of silence, remember? Lord of All knows, having that tongue of yours still for a time will be as much a miracle as us getting out of here without being spotted by your bedmate and Garnerius, or their men, but at least try to make it to the gates without it wagging."

Elsabeth glared at him but did not respond. True to Ehrhart's word the south range was deserted, and in a storage room at the end of the hall they found stacks of folded habits and cowls, all voluminous enough to disguise the telltale feminine curve of her figure, though one long enough for her height took a little more searching. The hedge separating the inner and outer courts was broken on all four sides with open archways, and as they stepped out of the south range, they found one of these passages directly across from them. With a cautious look up and down the inner court, Elsabeth and Hieronymus hurried through, before cutting to their left and making their way eastward along the hedge. They saw only a few servants tending the hedge and gardens in this part of the outer court, and no one stopped them as they hurried on their way. As they rounded the corner to head north, they saw the first sign of trouble; several armored men bearing halberds were scouring the grounds, stopping passersby and questioning them intently.

"Just keep walking, Tetty," Hieronymus muttered, "And keep quiet."

They ignored the soldiers and continued along their way, with Hieronymus setting a carefully measured pace to pass them as quickly as possible, while not obviously avoiding them. The soldiers appeared to be more interested in intimidating the various laypeople and paid them no mind. Elsabeth and Hieronymus soon passed them by, and as they made their way across the rest of the inner court to the main gate, they wove between buildings to avoid knots of other soldiers searching the grounds. They made it without incident, and as they approached the gate the gatekeeper met them with a reverent bow.

"Good day to you, Brothers," he said pleasantly. "There are some mighty strange goings on today."

Elsabeth cast back her cowl. "Yes, quite odd. Now then, I believe you have something that belongs to me."

The guard jumped in surprise. "Blasphemous wench—" he started, before seeing Hieronymus throw back his own hood. "What is the meaning of this?"

"We are cutting our visit to Alsfeld short," Hieronymus said. "Do be a good lad and fetch our weapons. Quickly and quietly, now, we would rather like to avoid a scene."

He nodded, his eyes still bewildered, and called up to his companion in the level above, through a cleverly-concealed grate Elsabeth now spied in the top of the gateway. A moment later the younger guard returned with their weapons cradled in his arms. Elsabeth snatched away her rondel and stuffed it through the cord belt of her habit, before reverently retrieving her sword and hanging the baldric over one shoulder, while Hieronymus reclaimed his sword and buckler. Hieronymus made the sign of the Wheel between him and the guard, and said, "Blessings of the Lord be upon you my son," then he took off briskly with Elsabeth close behind him, quickly pulling back up her hood and better securing her sword at her hip.

In the field just outside the gate they ran right into a hastily constructed encampment. The standard of Leyen, a white banner with a black dragon rampant, fluttered at the end of the poles marking the boundary of the camp. Horses were picketed neatly along one side away from the road, where plenty of grass was to be had, while a few of the soldiers milled about tending to the animals and gear. One or two stood guard, but leaned casually on their spears and showed little interest in their surroundings. The rest accompanied Cuncz and Garnerius into the monastery to search for the two fugitives.

"Well, that could be trouble in the near future," Elsabeth said as they made their way along the road. The soldiers in the camp showed no sign of making a move to stop them. "Even if they let us pass, they can overtake us easily once Garnerius and Cuncz realize we have slipped away."

"Hm, yes. We can always find a place for you to strip down and offer them a distraction, seeing as it worked so well against Lord Cuncz."

"Oh, very funny. Do you remember that bit of trouble we ran into in Erfurt?"

Hieronymus scowled. "Yes, quite well. As I recall I ended up naked in the town square tied to a lamppost."

"No! No, no, no, no, no, after that. Never, ever, speak of that again. The sight of that still gives me nightmares."

"Ah, yes, I see what you are getting at. I think it might work." Hieronymus turned away from the road and made his way toward the camp. Elsabeth adjusted her cowl to pull it low over her features as she followed him right up to the guards, who did not even straighten when they approached.

"Greetings, my sons," Hieronymus said, "and the blessings of the Lord be upon you."

"Good day, Father," one drawled. He leaned heavily on his spear. "What brings you out of your walls?"

"Thank you, but I am a humble brother only. Father Ehrhart asked that we see if anyone in your camp might need the services of a priest this day. My companion and I would be glad to take confession for you and your comrades."

"Kind of you to offer, Father," the soldier said, ignoring Hieronymus's correction of his office. He glanced at Elsabeth, but gave her no more than a cursory look. "You two expecting trouble or something? Tend not to see your sort bearing arms."

"Our teachings do extend to the noble art of defense, my son, and we were just on our way to Waldeck up the road at the request of one of the tradesmen to instruct his son. My companion is quite well versed in the style of Paulus von Soest, though I myself was a student of the great Leonardus in my youth. And as we were already due to be about, Father Ehrhart asked that we offer our services before we departed."

"We do appreciate it, Father. Some of us have not had a good confession in a stretch."

"Ah, then we shall begin right away! Brother Clement, do see about those good men tending to the horses, while I take confession here." Elsabeth bowed solemnly and made her way toward where the animals grazed. "You will need to pardon Brother Clement, he has taken a vow of silence so does not speak, but he can listen nonetheless," she heard Hieronymus explain as she slipped away in silence.

Though hastily set, and designed for quick abandonment at need, Elsabeth found the camp neat and arranged in quite an orderly fashion, with a clear demarcation between sleeping areas, latrines, and cooking fires. She easily threaded her way among the packs and bedrolls, and headed unerringly towards the lines of horses, enough for about two dozen men, picketed at the edge of the camp. She reached them without interruption and made a quick survey: The horses stood side by side in two groups, with one group behind the other, and each picket line tied between a pair of tall wooden stakes driven into the ground. The men left behind to tend the animals worked at the far end of the lines, and Elsabeth found herself left alone. The horses nearest her were still saddled and ready for riding, while the men at the far side worked their way down the line to remove their harnesses one by one. She smiled, and after a quick look about to make sure no one was near enough to see, ducked down and pulled both stakes at her end from the ground.

She chose the nearest two horses on the rear picket line and quickly untied them, then leading both a little ways away, drew her sword and swatted one of the other animals on the hindquarters and gave a sharp yell. The horse whinnied in alarm and bolted, taking the rest of the picket line with it. The other line startled as well, and soon the entire herd was stampeding away. A shout of alarm filled the camp as the soldiers took off after them, or sprung out of the way to avoid the crushing weight of the panicked animals, and Elsabeth used the time to cast off her habit and swing up into the saddle. She spurred the animal forward and charged through the living areas of the camp leading the second horse behind her, scattering tents, packs, and bedrolls, and nearly rode down the two men standing guard as they stood dumbstruck at the confusion erupting behind them. One spotted her and charged, but Hieronymus stuck his staff between his legs, and he tripped and tumbled to the ground in a heap. His companion went down from a quick blow to the teeth as Hieronymus quickly spun around to face him.

Elsabeth tossed the reins of the second horse to him, and he clambered up with an effort. "Well timed, Tetty," he said. "I do not think I could stomach another moment of their whining. You would think the Lord of All actually cared about every little impure thought that runs through a man's mind when a pretty girl walks by. Where to?"

"Back to Friuli," she said, and spurred her appropriated horse, with Hieronymus close behind. "If Cuncz was born there, there is sure to be a record of it, and maybe that will be enough to satisfy the Bishop and get us out of this mess."

She turned her horse up the road and they quickly left Alsfeld behind them.

Chapter X

The four-day walk between Friuli and Alsfeld passed much more quickly on horseback, pushing as hard as they dared, and stopping only well into the night to catch a few hours of sleep before resuming their ride just before daybreak. They reached the town a little after midmorning, with no sign of pursuit on the road behind them, and left their horses in the care of a communal stable just inside the gate, before making the rest of the trip to the Abbey on foot. They stood now, watching the gate, from a corner across the street.

"Well, here we are again," Hieronymus said as he stared up at the Abbey towering over the town. "Are you sure this is a good idea?"

"No," she said. "But I think I am rather out of good ideas at the moment."

"I have always wanted to visit Navarre."

"Somehow I doubt the Bishop's man will let us off so easily. There is always something to get us re-interested." Elsabeth folded her arms across her chest as she watched the gate and heaved a sigh. "Well, how do you want to do this? I for one, would rather like to avoid another climb up the privy shaft, especially in the middle of the day when it is more likely for someone to use it. And without knowing how long Garnerius and Cuncz will be delayed rounding up their horses, I think it best we not try to wait until dark."

"Well, I suppose that just leaves us the front door this time."

Hieronymus stepped around the corner and started across the street. Elsabeth quickly rearranged her sword to hang beneath her jacket, then hurried after to catch up and walk beside him. He regarded her with a slight roll of the eyes, but said nothing as they approached the gates. The guards waved them through with only a cursory looking over, Elsabeth fidgeting with her sword to better hide it from view. Hieronymus did not even bother to hide his from sight, and they were soon heading up the hill to the Abbey above.

The Abbey's layout was much the same as Alsfeld, though this church was larger, and with an even more opulent façade of imported white marble. The chapter house stood out notably on the east range with its peaked roof, and the second level housing the Abbot's private chambers rising above the rest of the range. Surrounding the complex were a large hospital, workshops, bakeries, guest houses, and storehouses. All were built in the same brick common throughout this part of Boehm, with tiled peaked roofs.

Hieronymus made for the west range, and as they entered were met by the cellarer, an older man with thin graying hair in a black habit. He bowed politely in greeting.

"Good morning, Brother," he said, "Blessings of the Lord be upon you. Is there something I may assist you with?"

"Yes," Hieronymus said after bowing in return, "My companion has a need to review the Abbey's records of births and deaths over the last thirty years."

The cellarer looked at Elsabeth uncertainly for a moment. "May I ask the purpose?"

"It is a personal matter," Elsabeth said.

"Ah," he said. "We typically do not allow the laity to view the Abbey records without the permission of Father Garnerius, who I regret has been called away from Friuli on business. However, he should return within the next few days…"

"Forgive me, Brother," Hieronymus said, "but I am afraid we do not have time for that." He glanced up at the ceiling and muttered, "Lord of All please forgive me for what I am about to do." Then he drew his sword and placed it at the throat of the cellarer, whose eyes widened in shock, but he admirably maintained his composure.

"If you will follow me, please," he said.

Elsabeth drew her rondel and placed it at the cellarer's back, while Hieronymus returned his sword to its scabbard. He led them out to the arcaded cloister, where a few brothers of the Abbey were gathered and spoke quietly among themselves. Elsabeth adjusted the sleeve of her jacket to cover her hand and dagger, and shifted around to the cellarer's side, while Hieronymus flanked him on the other. For his part, the man did not make a sound or give any indication to his brothers of anything out of the ordinary happening, and they passed without incident through the cloister and into the east range, which was currently deserted. He turned to his left, past the chapter house, and stopped before a door.

"The library is through here," he said calmly, the tip of the rondel still leveled at his side.

"Open it," Elsabeth firmly, and the cellarer did as instructed.

The library was a large room, extending well back from the outer wall of the east range, though not quite as large as the chapter house. Volumes of manuscripts lined the shelves, with a stepladder near at hand to reach the highest ones. Other books sat stacked on tables in the center of the room. A large and beautifully illuminated bible lay open on a pedestal near the door on their right as they entered, and there were also a few glass cases containing a wide array of artifacts. Along the wall on one side were a series of desks that served as workplaces, where a few scribes currently worked copying manuscripts. The *armarius* noticed their entrance and started toward them.

"Clear the room," Elsabeth ordered the cellarer quietly.

"Good morning, Brother," the *armarius* said in turn to Hieronymus and the cellarer as he reached them. "What may I do for you?"

"These good people have need of privacy while they consult our records," the cellarer said. If he gave any indication of his predicament, Elsabeth did not catch it.

The *armarius* frowned at Elsabeth and Hieronymus. "I was not aware anyone had been granted access to them, has Father Garnerius returned already?"

"I will discuss the matter with Father Garnerius when he returns," the cellarer said. "For the moment, I am convinced that these good people have need to view them, and they have requested privacy while they do."

The other regarded the cellarer for a moment, then sighed and nodded. "Very well, Brother." He turned to the scribes, who paused in their work to watch the commotion, and motioned them out. Elsabeth kept close to the cellarer, concealing her rondel between them, and as the last filed out Hieronymus closed the door behind them. There was no bolt or lock.

Elsabeth stepped away from the cellarer and returned her dagger to its sheath at her back. "We do apologize for this, but we really do not have much time." She swept her eyes around the shelves, and frowned when a system of organization was not readily apparent. "We need information on births and deaths recorded by the Abbey in the Spring of 1414," she said. "Where are they?"

"This way," the cellarer said, and led her to a shelf in the middle of the wall. He pulled the stepladder over, climbed up, and checked the spines of the books, then pulled down a large leather-bound volume. "Here it is. May I ask what this is all about, and why it is so important you would threaten violence in a house of the Lord?"

"I am sure the Lord of All will find it in His heart to forgive us if what we need is here," she said, but did not answer his question. She led the cellarer to a table, where he laid down the volume and opened it. "I presume it would be chronological by month?"

He nodded. "Yes, but the *armarius* would have better knowledge, I should go—"

As he started away, Elsabeth's hand shot out and snatched his robe. "No, you will stay right here. We can find it without his help." Elsabeth began paging through the entries line-by-line, each written in the same firm hand. The ink was somewhat faded, but the vellum pages were still clear. Most of the births and deaths were fairly ordinary; deaths from disease, age, conflict, or mishap, young children who passed after tragically short lives leaving grieving mothers and fathers, but then three entries all in a row caught her eye.

"Hieronymus," she said.

"What is it, Tetty?" he said as he approached to look over her shoulder. "You have something?"

"I think I might." She felt the cellarer lean in as well, as she pointed to the entries. "Two women were brought to the Abbey's infirmary due to difficult childbirths. Both died, as did one of the babies. The other survived."

"Hm. Lord Cuncz, do you think?"

"It could be, but that is not the most interesting thing about it: There is no information recorded about the woman whose child survived, but the other was a common woman by the name of Katherin from Dener."

"Dener is not far from Ortenau."

"Yes, and according to this Lord Emrich himself arranged the burial for both her and the child. Why would the Margrave pay for the burial of a peasant woman and her child?"

Hieronymus considered. "His mistress and bastard?"

Elsabeth nodded. "He must have felt some attachment to her. If she were a mere prostitute she would not even be a name in a book," she said, and tapped her finger on the other entry.

The cellarer leaned in over her shoulder to read the entry for himself, then shook his head. "That cannot be right," he said suddenly, and Elsabeth and Hieronymus both turned to him in surprise.

"What do you mean?" she said.

He studied the entry a moment longer. "I helped attend to Katherin Deners during the birth. It was a difficult one and she did not survive, but her child did."

Elsabeth's eyes widened. "Are you certain?"

The cellarer gave her an irritated look. "As God is my witness, I swear it to be true. The son of Katherin Deners survived. And as I recall, the other woman arrived perhaps a week later and bore a girl."

"Who made these entries?" Hieronymus asked.

"Father Garnerius always took it upon himself to enter the births and deaths."

"Bugger," Elsabeth said, her eyes going wide as saucers. "If I am right about this, that means Cuncz is Lord Emrich's bastard. He switched the children." She frowned thoughtfully. "But what would Father Garnerius have to gain in hiding this, or better yet, arranging for Lord Rupertus to adopt him?"

"Tetty, do you remember what land the Abbot had been buying up for Lord Cuncz?"

She shook her head. "Nothing particularly stands out, no."

"One was a small township not far from here. West of here. Friuli sits astride the border of the territories controlled by Ortenau to the west, and Leyen to the east. I think he was buying up land under Ortenau's influence adjacent to Friuli."

"But why?"

The cellarer cleared his throat. "Perhaps I can answer that, milady. Though mind you this is strictly idle gossip, and yes, even we at times fall victim to wagging tongues, but Father Garnerius and Lord Emrich have had a...strained relationship at best. They have had a number of political disagreements in the past, particularly where the extent of Friuli's influence has been concerned."

Elsabeth considered for a moment. "What would have happened had Lord Rupertus died without issue?"

He shrugged. "Lord Rupertus had no other kin to the best of my knowledge. I suppose the land would have reverted to his Grace the Prince-Bishop in Bremen, in the absence of an heir."

"And Bishop Augustin would likely redistribute the land as he saw fit. Possibly even to Lord Emrich. Oh, that is clever. Father Garnerius lets Emrich believe his child died during birth, and uses that same bastard to provide Lord Rupertus an heir to his lands and head off any attempt by Emrich to encircle Friuli."

Hieronymus nodded. "Which would make it rather difficult for Father Garnerius to expand his own political power. I suspect his Grace will wish to see those documents as well."

"Right," Elsabeth said, and with a cry of protest from the cellarer tore the page from the manuscript, folded it neatly, and stuffed it away inside her pouch. "Come on, best we not be here when the Abbot returns."

The words were no sooner from her mouth, then the door to the library burst open and four guards, armed with halberds, rushed in. Elsabeth's sword flashed as it cleared her scabbard, but she found herself trapped between the rows of tables running along the library floor and with no room to position herself for a fight. The *armarius* trailed after the guards as they entered, followed by Garnerius himself. The Abbot was a rather heavyset man with clean-shaven, scowling features, graying hair and blue eyes. He was dressed practically for the road in a travel-stained shirt, hose, and a doublet rather than in his robes of office. The cellarer showed deference immediately, but Elsabeth merely gripped her sword tighter and swept her gaze toward the guards, seeking for some means of escape.

"Well, you two have proven to be quite a bit of trouble," Garnerius said. He looked at her sword. "You would be wise to drop that. I would much prefer to not have to shed blood here."

Elsabeth ignored the implied threat. The reach of the halberds worked against them in such close quarters, though she doubted the tables would prove much of a barrier. "But you have no trouble with it in an inn at night if it is not by your hand," she said.

Garnerius chuckled. "Quite true, my child. There are, nonetheless, precedents we must now follow. You have assaulted the Baron of Leyen and his guards, stolen two horses, and forced entry into the Abbey. His Grace the Bishop will wish to have you tried before you are hung. But, by all means, resist arrest and die here. One way or another you will turn over everything you have found so this unfortunate mistake does not recur."

He motioned for the guards to advance, and Elsabeth took up a guard position and backed out from between the two tables on either side, and tried circling around to the north wall of the Library. Hieronymus's sword rang as he drew it and did the same, moving to the south in an effort to split the guards to where they could engage them one at a time. The guards advanced with care, taking their time to keep the pair from separating them.

Then a throaty chuckle filled the room as a familiar gravelly voice broke the building tension. "Well, what have we here? A whore, a friar, and an abbot all walk into an abbey. Hmm, I am sure you all have heard that one before, so let us forget the jokes." Out of the corner of her eye she saw the Hooded Man step through the doorway, followed by three guards bearing the livery of Leyen. Three guards with very familiar faces she was not quite able to place. "Call them off!" he said sharply to Garnerius, and waving at the Abbot's men.

Garnerius turned and glared at the cloaked and hooded figure approaching him from behind. "I beg your pardon? Have you any idea who you are addressing, my son?"

The man's voice changed, and suddenly became very smooth, cultured, and equally familiar. "Have you?" he said, and cast back his hood. Elsabeth's breath caught in her throat as she found herself gazing on Lord Cuncz, disguised by a fake beard, which he tore off and cast aside. He then turned his eyes on the Abbot's guards, who had halted their advancement at his entry, and now watched him uncertainly. "By order of his Grace the Bishop, Father Garnerius is to be arrested at once."

Garnerius's mouth dropped open in shock. Elsabeth lowered her sword, equally perplexed, as the guards eyed each other in shared confusion. "What is the meaning of this?" the Abbot said.

Cuncz flashed his lopsided smile. "Shall we start with attempted murder? Conspiracy? Or perhaps fraud? Really, Father, do you think you could have coerced the sale of all that land and someone would not notice?" He motioned to the guards. "Well, what are you waiting for? Take him away."

Garnerius sputtered furiously as the guards shrugged at each other and did as Lord Cuncz commanded. His own men — Elsabeth now recognized them as Jacobus, Clement, and Thadeus from the inn at Leyen — stepped forward to help escort the Abbot from the room. When the group had departed, Cuncz smiled and turned to the *armarius* and cellarer. "Leave us, if you will. And do see to it that you do not speak of what has happened in this room, thank you very much." The two did as he asked and hastily retreated from the library, leaving them alone.

"Ah, Elsabeth, or is it Gwenhevare? How wonderful it is to see you again. I do apologize for all that you have endured on my account, but unlike some others, I insist on seeing you both properly rewarded for your trouble."

She gawked, and it was a moment before Elsabeth found her voice. "What in God's name is going on here?"

He tsked and shook his head. "I can see you are rather confused, though I suspect you have reasoned out some of this on your own. You are quite a clever woman, after all. Something I find quite irresistible about you. His Grace the Bishop was suspicious of the Right Reverend Garnerius, particularly when Lord Emrich complained about the unusual amount of land he was coerced to turn over due to some financial mistakes made by his vassals that the good Abbot took advantage of." Cuncz stepped further into the library and headed toward her, looking over the books piled on the tables as he passed them. By now, Hieronymus had sheathed his sword, though Elsabeth kept hers loosely in hand as she watched the Baron approach. "You are wondering why I suppose?"

She nodded, eyeing him carefully. "That was the one question I have not exactly been able to answer."

"Father Garnerius's eye was not on Lord Emrich, although he certainly had little love for the man, but on his Grace himself. You see, he thought to set me up and use me as a powerbase against the Bishop, thinking me too disinterested in actually running Leyen to be a problem. Indirectly at first, of course, but I suspect he would take a more overt hand once he had the ability to do so, at which point he would find me rather expendable. I, of course, had plans of my own that did not involve being a tool in Garnerius's hand."

"So you cut a deal with the Bishop." She made it a statement of fact.

His smile broadened. "A new Abbot will need to be appointed over Friuli, and will be made a vassal of Leyen. And I get to keep the property Father Garnerius so thoughtfully acquired for me. We both make out quite nicely, I would say; his Grace rids himself of a potential rival, and I gain Friuli and a bit of Lord Emrich's land. I did find myself needing to improvise a tad when the two of you spoiled the theft I arranged, but no harm done in the end. Now then..." he extended his hand toward her. "If you would be so kind as to return my property. Oh! And also that page I believe you took from the Abbey's records, I would rather like to see that such inconvenient documents are kept somewhat safer. And I promise you will not be needing that," he added with a nod at her sword.

Elsabeth watched him for a moment, sighed, and reluctantly returned her sword to its scabbard. "You mentioned a reward?" she said searchingly, as she reached into her pouch and retrieved the documents she lifted from Cuncz's study, and the page from the Abbey's records. She handed them over to Cuncz, who did not even bother disguising it when he checked to ensure they were all there, and watched him expectantly.

"Yes, of course," he said absently, then folded the pages and stuffed them inside his cloak. Cuncz untied a pouch from his belt and tossed it to Hieronymus. "For your parish, Brother. Though I suspect a goodly amount will be donated to the nunneries between here and there. And if you would do me the courtesy of giving me a moment alone with your companion?"

"Tetty?" Hieronymus said, as he checked the contents of the purse and slipped the coin back in again.

Elsabeth nodded toward the door. "Go on, if he has anything untoward planned I can handle it."

They watched him go, and as he shut the door behind him Elsabeth folded her arms across her chest and gazed levelly at Cuncz. "You knew. The entire time I was in Leyen; at dinner, in bed, you knew who I really was."

Cuncz's smile broadened, and it was as self-satisfied an expression as Elsabeth had ever seen. "Of course."

"I could have killed you, you know. Perhaps I could have misjudged the dose when I drugged you, or that might have been poison in your wine altogether. Or I could have just cut your throat."

"Sweet Tetty, the risk was part of what made our encounter so exhilarating. Of course, no matter what you would have done, I intended to see to it you did not leave Leyen without those documents one way or another. Assuming I had not been killed of course, in which case you would never have escaped. I had my men, which you did recognize them just now I believe. Perhaps I shall introduce you properly in the future, but suffice to say, they are my most trusted bodyguards, and were every bit as skeptical about such a plan as no doubt your own companion was. Well, I had them suggest a very simple and hopefully pleasurable course of action," he said, and scooped up her hand. "And I did mean what I said that night: You are a rare beauty, and I could hardly let you pass through my walls without sampling everything your charms had to offer." He kissed the back of her fingertips, and Elsabeth blushed fiercely in spite of herself.

"You sly bastard," she said.

He flashed that lopsided smile again. "The only trouble I find myself in, is having had a taste, I cannot resist the thought of having more. I would very much like you to come back to Leyen with me, as my mistress. You would be provided for and would no longer need to scrape a living on the road in the dangerous sort of work you do now. And perhaps I could use my not inconsiderable influence to arrange to make our relationship a truly respectable one in the future. It would need to be a lesser title, perhaps, and not right away, but in time."

Elsabeth's stomach fluttered a bit, but she pushed him to arm's length and regarded him with a smirk of her own. "And it keeps me close by where you can keep an eye on me, so I cannot let it slip just what has been going on here without you knowing of it immediately."

He chuckled. "I see it will not be quite so easy to fool you in the future. That thought does occur to me, yes. But I must say, I am rather smitten with you." Cuncz heaved a sigh. "I do not think I can ever look at another woman again without comparing her to you."

She blushed and gave him a gentle peck on the lips, and slipped past him to give herself a clean line for the door in the event he did not take her rejection well. "I will not deny that I will be remembering our little tryst rather fondly on many lonely nights to come, but I think it would be more in my interest to not be under your roof should you decide me to be an inconvenience."

Cuncz caught her hand again and pulled her back to him. "Do not think for a moment that I intend to accept defeat yet, but if that is your decision for now, I will not think to dishonor it by giving you an ultimatum." The lopsided smile flashed across his lips again. "And I think I will quite enjoy the chase, and find claiming the quarry that much sweeter in the end." He kissed her long and deeply. Elsabeth closed her eyes and let a soft moan escape, and just before she pulled away, she felt something pressed into the palm of her hand. They parted, and in her hand was a gold ring set with a faceted red stone. "For you, pretty." He stroked her chin with his thumb. "Do take care of yourself; I expect to see you again."

Elsabeth let out a giddy laugh as she backed away from him and slipped the ring into a pouch on her belt. "Oh, I will. But I think I best be on my way before Hieronymus leaves me behind, or you change your mind about letting me just walk away. Do give my regards to the Bishop."

And then she quickly slipped from the library and left him behind.

"So did you defile the library?" Hieronymus said as she caught up with him making his way south along the east range.

"Oh, do you really think so little of me?" she said.

Hieronymus merely grunted. "So where to now?"

"Far from here, I think." She flashed him a smirk. "I have always wanted to visit Navarre."

He chuckled. "I am sure there are plenty of places for us to get in trouble along the way."

"Doubtless, so at least the road will be entertaining. Come on, let us be off."

Presenting a first look at the next adventure of Elsabeth Soesten…

Bait And Switch

Chapter 1

Her longsword flashed from its scabbard as the blur of something rather large and heavy flying towards her caught her eye, and in one fluid movement Elsabeth spun away from her horse and cut the melon aimed at her head neatly in two, its halves spinning off harmlessly away from her in a shower of juice and pulp that splattered in a broad streak across her heart-shaped face. She was not exactly certain from which direction the missile came, but judging from the angry faces and chorus of curses raining down on her from the villagers approaching her, she needed no specifics. If her deft defense against the unexpected attack startled any of the crowd they did not show it, and if anything the failed assault only enraged them further. Especially evident when a hasty shower of stones followed the melon that sent her scrambling to the far side of the horse, though none of these carried nearly so far nor as accurately as the melon.

Hieronymus, his portly round face framed by his unruly mane of graying hair, clutched his carved wooden staff and stepped between Elsabeth and the crowd, pleading for their attention. "Peace, sons and daughters, peace!" he said in his passable Navarrese, touched with a heavy Boehman accent. "Do not give in to wrath. Remember what the Son of the Lord would say of forgiveness!"

Neither the travel- and ale-stained black woolen habit of his order nor the sword and buckler hung at his hip made an impression on the crowd, and a hail of insults answered him, most directed at her to judge by the count of "whores" and "harlots" screamed by the women of the village, and another ragged volley of stones aimed past the friar and in her direction that fell harmlessly short. The men mostly kept to the rear of the crowd and well out of the way, more than a few with looks of utter embarrassment on their faces. The village priest, a handsome man somewhat younger than her twenty-three summers and dressed in a brown woolen habit, stepped forward to join the fat friar and to mediate the situation. "I beg of you, my children," he said, "let justice prevail, not anger. If this woman has wronged you then let the Lord of All cast his judgment and she will be punished accordingly."

He turned to Elsabeth. "My child, will you come forward?" he said, and Hieronymus looked at her as well as if looking for her response. She gave the slightest hint of a nod towards his horse, and Hieronymus slowly inched his way over to his own animal. "There need not be any violence if you will consent to answer to their charges."

Elsabeth wiped the melon pulp from her face with one elbow and swept the tail of her brown leather longcoat back behind her hip to clear her scabbard, then sheathed her sword. She flashed the priest a mischievous smirk, and an amused sparkle filled her green eyes. "Oh, there is no need for that," she said, her own Navarrese was mostly clean with little in the way of an accent. She touched her heart. "Bless me father, for I have indeed sinned, and lain with several men of the village. And if the women here are as skilled in their beds as they are at flinging stones, then it is small wonder I found the men so willing."

Hieronymus rolled his eyes at her when he reached his horse, and a fresh volley of stones, curses, insults and oaths filled the village. "Well that will certainly smooth things over," he said in Boehman as he hurried to ready his own horse.

"We already got paid for the job," she said in a low voice, "so there is no need to come back again, anyway. Let us just go before they light the torches."

The priest managed to contain the crowd again with great effort, and turned back to her. "I beg of you, my child," he said. "For the good of your soul you must make amends to those whom you have wronged!"

Elsabeth tsked at him. "Oh father, and I thought my soul was already in such good hands when I was on my knees before you last night. I would think all of Navarre heard your prayers with the way you were carrying on."

The priest's face turned a brilliant shade of crimson, and for a moment he sputtered and could not find the words for a rebuke. "Harlot! Succubus!" he finally spat, and pointed at her accusatorily. "There for certain stands a servant of the Dark One himself! See how her tongue weaves salacious lies?"

"Well now you did it, Tetty," Hieronymus muttered.

"Yes," she said, "I may have pushed this one a tad too far."

"In the name of the Lord, seize the witch so she might be burned, and her corruption lifted from our village!" the priest said.

"Time to go?" Hieronymus said.

Elsabeth vaulted into the saddle. "Time to go!"

As the townsfolk surged forward—the men now gladly joining the pursuit in hopes that having a scapegoat to burn would wash away their own indiscretions—Elsabeth gave a cry and jammed her heels into the horse's flanks. She sped away from the village, copper hair streaming behind her like a gleaming banner, with only a look over her shoulder to be sure Hieronymus was with her and to check for signs of pursuit. However their horses were fine and swift coursers, and swiftly left behind the villagers, who had only their hacks and packhorses with which to attempt a pursuit

They rode hard for several miles, and only when the village lay well behind them hidden by a turn of the road as it passed through a small wooded area did she pull up her horse and check her pace. Hieronymus rode up beside her and shook his head. "Well, that was another fine mess you got us into," he said.

"Me?" she said. "This whole adventure was yet another of your mad schemes I got dragged along on to keep you out of trouble."

"Yes, you. God in heaven, girl, what has gotten into you lately? I have seen you leave a trail of broken hearts—and I suspect very angry wives—from one end of Boehm to the other, but this has been excessive even for you. Did you lay with every man there or just the ones whose wives were throwing stones?"

"It was actually only two of them. Well, and the priest, but he was a strange one, and insisted only that I—"

He cut her off abruptly. "Enough, girl, enough! That is all I really can bear to hear, especially so long as you continue to refuse my own advances."

She rolled her eyes. "You did bring it up."

"Only because you nearly got yourself burned at the stake for it. And likely me with you. Now something has been bothering you ever since we crossed into the Navarre. I am your priest, such as it is, am I not?"

Elsabeth eyed him incredulously. "Are you saying you want me to give confession now?"

"Who said anything about confession? I am merely offering you the comfort of my ear. And I rather hope you take advantage of it before the next village you scandalize sees fit to lock up our only means of escape before coming to hang you."

She sighed again. "If you must know, though it is rather none of your business, it has been nigh on six weeks since I have had satisfaction by means other than my own hands, and I am trying very hard not to think of Lord Cuncz and his magic wand. I am likely to get more enjoyment from bumping along in the bloody saddle than from any man I have had of late. And now here I am telling you about it on top of it all."

"I happen to think it is a message. For too long you have willingly opened your body to any man with a pulse. The Lord of All does not wish to see you flitting from bed to bed like a common whore, it is unbecoming."

Elsabeth rolled her eyes at him. "And what does He say about the high regard you show to your vows, hypocrite? I am sure He thinks highly of the sort of 'indulgence' you offer the laywomen."

Hieronymus harrumphed and looked towards the sky as he bobbed along in the saddle. "Lord, grant me patience with your wayward daughter! I offer her advice and she responds by questioning my piety!"

"Your piety deserves questioning, and you well know it. Nor did I ask for your advice, particularly if it is of the sort you decided to force upon me. The sort of bed I make to lie in is none of your concern, so if you do not like it you can go and bugger yourself."

At that they rode in silence for some time, and after a mile or so they passed through the wooded area and broke out into open fields stretching out for some distance in all directions. No sign of pursuit followed them, and they passed no one else on the road, though at times they saw peasants at work in the fields. The road was a rutted and hard-packed dirt track that ran with a slightly meandering path in a southwesterly direction, and was at times crossed by little streams gurgling in stony beds passed by ford or bridges of crumbling and weathered stone. Here and there they saw the remains of old paving stones peeking through the dirt and turf like old bleached bones, a rare sign of the great empire that once stretched out of the Free City-States to the south, to cover much of Navarre and Coventry further to the northeast.

It was already midday by the time they set out from the village, and it promised to be well after twilight before they reached their destination, which Elsabeth noted Hieronymus had not been forthcoming about. Finally she could take no more of riding with only the singing of birds and the steady clatter of their horses' hooves to break the silence.

"Where are you taking us, anyway," she said.

"Somewhere to get a drink, and maybe a bit of work to keep you occupied and out of trouble, though you seem to have a knack for drawing it wherever you go."

She rolled her eyes. "Any time you go looking for a drink and a bit of work I always end up having to get you out of trouble. Like that time you tried to hustle those gents in Aue and ended up hung by your ankles from the village church."

"That was not my fault! They were easy marks, and I would have had them if you would have just done as I asked."

"I love it when my sleeping habits are suddenly much less objectionable once you think you can use them to your advantage. The man was a disgusting pig and I do have standards. Now what are you planning this time?"

"My plan was to head for a place a bit up the road the priest back there," he jerked his thumb over his shoulder, motioning vaguely back towards the village, "mentioned before your 'standards' triggered a riot. He called it the Inn of the Four Ways."

Elsabeth let out a groan of exasperation. "Oh good God, not another inn. Why is it always a bloody inn?"

"Do you know of anywhere better to look for someone needing a sword-arm or two? The Four Ways is right at a major crossroads so anyone on the road will be passing through. I am sure there will be no lack of merchants and travelers looking for protection on the road."

"And it is also a good place for you to lose all our money on drink and dice. How long did it take before you had been through your share of the reward from Cuncz?"

Hieronymus glared at her. "As I recall you enjoyed your fair share of the libations along the road, Tetty. Every innkeeper between here and Leyen I am sure has been singing your praises after we pass through. Not to mention your name, among other things, has been on the lips of probably every bard and minstrel as well. Now will you just trust me? I know what I am doing."

She sighed and shook her head. "It scares me every time you say that."

The rest of their ride was uneventful. Midday passed into afternoon, and soon the sun was beginning to sink into the west, setting the sky alight with brilliant golds and reds as the pale blue ceiling overhead slowly deepened into indigo, and the silver-white points of stars ignited in the gathering dark. The sun was nothing more than a red half-globe peeking above the dark rim of the horizon when the golden lights of their destination loomed up ahead of them.

The Inn of the Four Ways was a substantial structure nestled in the northeast corner of the joining of the two roads whence it took its name. The greater of the two ran north and south across Navarre, and was worn and deeply rutted by the passage of merchant wagons. The road Elsabeth and Hieronymus followed westward from Boehm was less well-traveled in these days, though once had been a major passage for goods moving overland. In summer months the hard dirt surfaces were a sea of choking dust, making the Four Ways a welcome respite to travelers.

The Inn was virtually a town in of itself, enclosed within a wooden gated palisade atop a low grassy rise overlooking the road, backed by a small wooded area with a clear bright pond beside it. A broad path branched off the north-south road to run up to the main gate to the south, and bisected the grounds behind the wall before exiting another gate on the north face and eventually rejoining the main highway. Brightly-painted homes and shops lined both sides of this path within the walls, with merchant stalls and several open squares, dominated by the Inn itself at its heart.

The Inn straddled the path, with a long two-leveled wing with peaked roofs and many windows on each side connected by a central section through which the road passed by means of an archway. Beneath this section were also stables and stalls for the sheltering of horses, and a doorway in each corner led inside. Buildings clustered around it to create a maze of alleys, and there were many merchant stalls to take advantage of the heavy traffic as travelers sought the shelter of its roof or the comfort of its tables.

Elsabeth left Hieronymus to arrange the stabling of their horses and to secure lodgings for the night, and disappeared into the maze of market stalls, which were still active as night descended on the Inn. Lamps cast golden light across an open square encircled by a mass of bodies pressing in to watch jugglers performing for the crowd while pick-pockets worked the distracted spectators.

Music and voices rose in a sonorous roar while the aroma of cooking food from the many stalls clashed in the evening air, and even in the fading light merchants continued to hawk their wares with bold displays and boisterous calls. It took her little time and subtle inquiry to find the stall she sought, and she was soon making her way back to the Inn with a bundle stuffed inside her jacket.

She entered through the door in the southeast corner of the central wing, and found herself on a well-lit landing at the foot of a steep stairway. Golden light filled the room above, and there was music and the aroma of cooking food and the sour odor of beer on the air. Elsabeth started up the stairs and soon emerged in the inn's common room, a wide chamber that filled the entirety of the middle section of the Inn above the stables below. Glass windows looked north and south out onto the road, and thick timber columns supported the ceiling above. A stairwell at each corner of the common room led down to an entrance like the one she entered through, while a door on either end led to the east and west wings, which housed the Inn's lodgings.

Trestle tables ringed an open space in the middle of the common room floor, where men and women danced to a jaunty tune played by musicians on pipes, drums and lutes, while serving girls glided between tables and spun out of the reach of grasping hands. Elsabeth flashed one of the pipers a smile when he looked her way, then swept her eyes across the common room. She found Hieronymus tucked away in a table near the southwest stairwell. She sighed and made her way across the room to join him, keeping to the wall and out of the way as she slipped past tables full of drinkers, some stained and worn from the road, and locals come to the Inn to share news of the day and to join in the revelry of the evening.

She reached him and dropped heavily onto the bench, propping her sword against the table and happy for the moment to take a seat that was not constantly moving beneath her.

"Did you find what you were looking for?" Hieronymus asked. He leaned over a platter of warm bread and stewed meat, with a tankard of ale at his elbow.

"Not that it is any of your business, but yes I did," she said. Elsabeth pulled the small bundle, little more than a plain linen pouch wrapped in twine, from her jacket and dropped it on the table. Before long a serving girl appeared bearing a platter of the evening's meal and a tankard of ale for her, which she set down with an uncertain eye on the sword leaning against the table. Elsabeth handed her the linen bundle and a piece of silver.

"Be a dear and have this boiled into tea for me," she said.

The serving girl inclined her head slightly and hurried off to the kitchens. A few minutes into her meal the girl returned with a pewter teapot and a small clay cup, and set them both on the table with a bow.

"Thank you, love," Elsabeth said, and the girl bowed once more and hurried off to see to other patrons. Elsabeth gingerly lifted the pot and poured herself a cup. The tea was very hot and bitter to the taste, and she made a face as she drank it. "God I hate this stuff."

"Serves you right, Tetty," Hieronymus said.

"Oh do not start with me again. So what do you have in mind? Are we just sitting around and waiting for someone to show up?"

Hieronymus took a long draught of his ale and wiped his mouth on the sleeve of his habit. "More or less."

Elsabeth sighed and rolled her eyes. "Wonderful. We could just spend the night at ease and move on somewhere that work would actually posted. Instead we hang around just hoping for something to turn up on its own. Brilliant plan."

"Show some faith, my girl, and do keep your sword in view."

She took another drink of her tea, scowled at the cup, and shook her head. "Fine. But I wager our meal and board for the night that nothing turns up."

Hieronymus smirked over the rim of his tankard. "Wager accepted."

ABOUT THE AUTHOR

D. E. Wyatt was born and lives in St. Louis, Missouri. When not writing he studies Medieval German swordsmanship.

31479510R00079

Printed in Great Britain
by Amazon